Colt noticed a flash of something off in the trees. Sunlight bouncing off a rifle scope?

"Get down!" He leaped forward and jerked Morganne's arm, yanking her off her feet at the exact same moment gunfire echoed around them.

"What in the world...?" Morganne gasped.

"Shooter is straight ahead. Get behind the SUV." He practically dragged her with him to the shelter of the vehicle. He pulled out his phone and dialed 911 to report the gunfire.

"If that's Blaine, we need to go after him," Morganne said in a low voice.

"Not when he has a rifle with a scope. Too easy for him to pick us off."

"We can't just sit here," Morganne protested. "We have to do something."

He understood and shared her need to find the shooter. But not while they were sitting ducks. If the shooter was Blaine, the guy had gone on the attack.

The hunter had just become the hunted.

Laura Scott has always loved romance and read faith-based books by Grace Livingston Hill in her teenage years. She's thrilled to have been given the opportunity to retire from thirty-eight years of nursing to become a full-time author. Laura has published over thirty books for Love Inspired Suspense. She has two adult children and lives in Milwaukee, Wisconsin, with her husband of thirty-five years. Please visit Laura at laurascottbooks.com, as she loves to hear from her readers.

Books by Laura Scott

Love Inspired Suspense

Justice Seekers

Soldier's Christmas Secrets
Guarded by the Soldier
Wyoming Mountain Escape
Hiding His Holiday Witness
Rocky Mountain Standoff
Fugitive Hunt

Alaska K-9 Unit

Tracking Stolen Secrets

Visit the Author Profile page at LoveInspired.com for more titles.

FUGITIVE HUNT

LAURA SCOTT

LOVE INSPIRED SUSPENSE
INSPIRATIONAL ROMANCE

ISBN-13: 978-1-335-73613-0

Fugitive Hunt

For questions and comments about the quality of this book, please contact us at CustomerService@Harlequin.com.

Love Inspired
22 Adelaide St. West, 41st Floor
Toronto, Ontario M5H 4E3, Canada
www.LoveInspired.com

Printed in U.S.A.

But thanks be to God, which giveth us the victory
through our Lord Jesus Christ.

—1 Corinthians 15:57

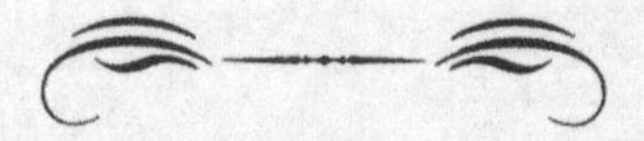

This book is dedicated to my critique group,
Lori Handeland, Oliva Rae and Pamela Ford.
You guys are the best!

ONE

When Jackson, Wyoming, police officer Morganne Kimball's cell phone rang at four in the morning, she knew it was bad news. Nothing good happened at this hour. She blindly felt for the phone and managed a hoarse "Kimball."

"Blaine Winston was sighted in Jackson six hours ago."

The news from her boss, Lieutenant Jerome Graves, had her bolting upright in bed. "Six hours? And I'm just hearing now? When? Where? Who saw him?"

"Unfortunately, I don't have a lot of information," the lieutenant said. "And for all we know, it's another mistake. You know how people are. They want to help but often only cause more work for law enforcement, forcing us to follow up on bad information."

She dragged a hand through her tangled red hair, knowing her boss was right. Five years ago, Blaine Winston had murdered three girls and had almost killed a fourth. Her. Unfortunately, he'd escaped from federal prison nine months ago during an ambulance crash that was likely staged with outside help, and he'd then disappeared without a trace. Everyone, including her, assumed that Blaine had fled the country, heading down into Mexico or up to Canada.

"Apparently a bartender at a local tavern thought he recognized Winston," her boss continued. "The information went to the Feds first, who then informed us. But again, we don't know how reliable this guy's testimony is. The man he saw may not be your cousin."

Your cousin. She didn't need the reminder that she shared blood with the infamous killer from whom she'd escaped and whom she'd helped capture. Blaine Winston was her dad's sister's son, about six years her senior. Thanks to her ability to escape and bring him down, Blaine had been sentenced to life without parole in the prison in Laramie.

At least, that's where he should be.

For nine months now, she'd worried about Blaine being free to return to his murdering ways. She often woke up in a cold sweat, reliving those moments when he'd grabbed her from behind, nearly choking her.

Before she could ask anything further about the so-called witness, the motion sensor floodlights abruptly flashed on, bathing the entire backyard of her house in light.

All her cop instincts went on high alert. "I have to go. My back floodlights just came on."

Without waiting for her boss's response, she disconnected the call, slipped from the bed and eased toward the window. Despite the recent sighting of Blaine, she didn't really think he was out there. But she wasn't making rash assumptions, either.

Blaine had sent her numerous letters from prison in the early days after his arrest, vowing to seek revenge for getting him arrested. Of course the deputies confiscated the letters, providing her the gist of their contents, which was that Blaine wanted to finish what he'd started.

He wanted to kill her.

With the lights still illuminating her yard, Morganne backed away from the window. She quickly pulled on jeans and a hoodie, stuffed her feet into running shoes, and grabbed her service weapon. Moving along the wall, she peered through the window again, searching for signs of someone being out there. Her lights often flashed on when animals passed by. She'd caught glimpses of deer, antelope, coyotes and even the occasional bear. Logically it made sense that an animal had triggered them now, rather than some sort of intruder. Still, her stomach knotted as she thought about Blaine's promise to seek revenge.

He'd escaped nine months ago. Why come after her now? Why not just take his freedom and move on? It didn't make any sense to her that he'd risk the possibility of being captured just to satisfy a grudge.

Unfortunately, Blaine considered himself smarter than everyone else around him. He might just be arrogant enough to come here and attempt to kill her, feeling certain he could slip away once again.

The outside lights shut down, the sensors no longer picking up movement. She didn't relax but continued to look out the window to see if anyone was out there.

Crack!

She instinctively turned away from the window as it shattered beneath the force of a bullet. Hitting the floor, she crawled across the room to the bedroom door. She felt like a sitting duck inside the house.

She needed to get out, where she would be better able to defend herself.

Desperately wishing for a pair of night-vision goggles, Morganne crawled to the kitchen. She eyed the car keys on the counter but decided against using them to drive away. The garage door would rise far too slowly, giving the intruder time to attack.

Instead, she headed down to the basement to flip the breaker and shut down the supply of electricity to the floodlights. She needed them to remain off if she was going to go out there to find the gunman. As she went, she called for backup, citing gunfire on her property. The dispatcher promised to send squads, but she wasn't going to wait.

Morganne wasn't some damsel in distress. Five years ago she'd vowed to never be a victim again. She'd become a cop and held her own, in spite of her male counterparts underestimating her.

The same way Blaine had underestimated her.

She scrambled back to the main level and eased outside her front door, keeping her back to the house and sweeping her gaze over the area.

The front of her property faced the road, and there were a few houses across the street, although they were spaced out rather than crowded together like some neighborhoods in Jackson. Along the back of her lot was a small wooded area.

No doubt that was where the gunman had hidden. Yet he must have gotten close enough to her backyard to trigger the lights.

As she moved down toward the corner of her house, she heard a voice.

"Kimball."

She spun with her weapon up, ready to shoot, when she recognized a man with short blond hair, topped by a cowboy hat with a five-point star pinned to his chest. She recognized him as US Marshal Colt Nelson.

"I almost shot you," she whispered

harshly. "What are you doing here, Nelson?"

"Following up on the sighting of Winston." His gaze was serious. "From the sound of gunfire, I think we may have found him."

Fugitive apprehension was one of the roles of the US Marshals, but she didn't appreciate his showing up at her house without warning. "Did you see him?"

"No. I was setting up to watch your place when the floodlights turned on. I don't think he was expecting that, and frankly, neither was I. After the lights went on, I was about to make my way around back when I heard the shot and the sound of glass breaking."

For a fraction of a second, she doubted the timing of his story, but then she shook off her suspicions. She'd helped Colt and several other US Marshals on a case last June and had found the marshals to be honest and hardworking.

Besides, it was easy to believe Nelson

was here to find Winston. Although she wished the Feds had clued in the locals earlier. "You should have let me know you were out here. I hit the breaker switch, so the lights won't go on."

"Smart move." He sounded impressed by her actions. Which didn't say much for his opinion of her skills as a cop, but she let that slide.

"We need to split up and see if we can flush him out." She eyed Colt, judging his reaction to her suggestion.

He hesitated, then slowly nodded. "Okay, but let me call for backup."

She shot him an exasperated glance. "I already did that. We can't wait—he may already have taken off. You go left, I'll go right and we'll see if we can pin him down somewhere in the middle. If he's still here, he'll be hiding in the wooded section of my property. And we already know he's armed and dangerous." Even if the shooter wasn't Blaine, the fact that the perp had shot at her bedroom window was an indication that he or she intended to cause serious harm, without caring who was caught in the crossfire.

Colt gave a curt nod, indicating he was on board with her plan. She turned and quickly made her way to the corner of the house. She paused to listen. To Colt's credit, she didn't hear him at all.

Easing forward, she continued to the next corner, pausing to sweep another gaze over her backyard.

Morganne had chosen this particular house because of the dense cluster of trees all along the back of the lot line, providing her privacy along with a sense of being close to nature.

There was thirty yards of grass, the ground now muddied from the May rains, before the wooded area began.

Thirty yards of open space where she could be easily picked off by an expert marksman.

Blaine wasn't an expert at shooting, although most men in Wyoming were taught at an early age how to shoot a gun. Still, she knew full well Blaine preferred killing his victims by strangling them.

Which made her question if he was really the one out there hiding in the dark.

Regardless, she needed to move. She sucked in a deep breath and abruptly pushed away from the house. She sprinted across the open space, mentally braced for the impact of a bullet.

Upon reaching the shelter of the trees, she dropped into a crouch and attempted to calm her racing heart. Still hearing nothing, she eased slowly through the brush. The good news was that this was her place. She knew the wooded area very well. More so than a stranger.

A good three minutes passed as she made her way silently through the trees. When she caught a glimpse of movement up ahead, she quickly lifted her weapon. Only to lower it again when she recognized Colt.

Colt wore a grim expression as he shook

his head. She frowned. The wooded area wasn't that large, but he couldn't have searched and cleared it that quickly.

Then she heard a car engine rumbling loud in the silence of the night.

The shooter? No! He was getting away!

She bolted from the woods, running flat out toward the road. Just in time to see a dark square-shaped vehicle without lights disappearing from view.

She groaned and bent at the waist, breathing heavily.

They'd lost him.

Colt came up to stand beside Morganne. "You okay?"

"No." Her response was curt as she straightened. "He shouldn't have gotten away."

"But you're not hurt?" he pressed. Losing his quarry didn't make him feel good, either, but he was more concerned about her being injured. "I thought I saw blood on your cheek."

She brushed at her face, smearing the blood. "Probably hit by glass when the window shattered. Do you really think that was Blaine? I mean, this isn't his MO."

He nodded. "You're right about that. I wasn't expecting to hear gunfire. I would have thought he'd try to enter your house in some way, to attack while you were sleeping. But the lights flashing on may have changed his plans. And it could be that your cousin wants you dead so badly he'll use any means available to him." He gestured to the road as a couple of squads pulled up. "Here's the cavalry, better late than never."

"It doesn't make sense Blaine would come back here after being off the radar for nine months."

He agreed with her assessment. "Does that mean you have someone else out there who wants you dead? An ex-boyfriend, ex-husband, maybe?"

"Don't be ridiculous." She lifted her

chin. "I've never been married and don't have a man in my life."

Personally, Colt couldn't understand why not. Morganne was very attractive, slim and tall for a woman, with beautiful, silky red hair and clear gray eyes.

He remembered her from a case he and two of his fellow marshals, Tanner Wilcox and Slade Brooks, had worked in June of last year. Slade's witness had been shot at his own wedding, and as they'd kept the bride safe, they had uncovered a dirty cop on the Jackson police force. Thanks to her quick thinking and solid cop instincts, Morganne had saved the lives of both his friends Duncan and Chelsey.

Arriving here in time to hear the gunfire had disturbed him. When he'd come to stake out her house hoping for Blaine Winston to show up, he hadn't expected bullets to fly.

"Wait a minute," he said as he realized what he'd just considered. "What ever happened to that former lieutenant? The one who was secretly working for Travis Wolfe?"

"Goldberg went to jail." Morganne didn't even look at him as she moved forward to greet the officers who'd come onto the scene. She rose her voice so they could hear her. "I'm Officer Kimball. Someone fired a gun at my bedroom window. US Marshal Nelson and I tried to find the shooter, but he escaped."

Colt hung back, letting her take the lead. It was, after all, her house. And he was only here because he was assigned to apprehend the escaped fugitive.

Three women had died at Winston's hands, and Morganne herself had been his fourth victim. The one who'd gotten away. He'd heard Winston could be carrying a grudge against women who reminded him of his mother. Four victims, yet Colt felt certain there were others they didn't know about. Especially considering the nine months Winston had been on the run.

"Marshal? We'd like to take your statement about what happened here."

Colt glanced up at the officer standing in front of him. He noted the guy's name tag identified him as Jamison. "No problem."

He proceeded to succinctly explain why he'd come and what he'd heard. "I did not see the shooter, unfortunately. Officer Kimball and I went around to clear the backyard, especially the wooded area along the back of her property, but we didn't find anything. That's when we heard the vehicle start up. By the time we reached the road, the car was disappearing from view."

"Make or model?" Jamison asked.

He remembered a boxy shape. "Maybe a Jeep, or a van. But I couldn't say for certain. The driver didn't use lights, so it was impossible to see specific details."

"I understand you're here following up on a tip about Blaine Winston being in the area. Do you think he's responsible for this?"

"Maybe, but since neither one of us saw the shooter's face, there's no way to know for sure." Colt glanced at his watch. He needed to check in with his boss about this latest incident, see if any other information had come in about Winston. "I have things to do." He handed the cop his business card. "You can reach me at this number if you need anything."

"Hold on a minute," Jamison protested as he tried to step around him. "You really think it's possible the shooter was Winston and that Officer Kimball was the intended target? If he'd escaped law enforcement for the past nine months, why come after her now?"

Colt suppressed a sigh. "I don't know. It's just one theory, but that's what I'm hoping to find out."

Jamison frowned. "Yeah, okay."

Colt continued walking. He'd purposefully left his own SUV several yards down the road so as not to tip anyone off to his presence.

Fat lot of good that had done.

"Marshal Nelson? Colt? Wait up!"

He turned to find Morganne jogging toward him. The cut on her cheek wasn't deep, but seeing the blood marring her beautiful skin bothered him.

"Do you need something?" He stopped and faced her. "I can help board up your broken window."

"Where are you going?" Her eyes flashed with anger.

"I need to continue searching for your cousin."

"Stop calling him that," she snapped. "Do you think I appreciate having a killer in the family? That my own flesh and blood attacked me? Nearly killed me?"

"I'm sorry." He winced inwardly, regretting his words. He wouldn't want to be reminded about a blood tie to someone like Winston, either. "I should check in with my boss and talk to the witness who claimed to see Winston. I need to hit the road."

"Give me a few minutes to change, and I'll be ready to go."

He blinked and tipped the brim of his cowboy hat up to see her face more clearly. He met her gaze head-on. "I'm sorry, but you really don't have any jurisdiction in this matter. You're a local cop, Morganne, and this is a federal case. Besides, we don't even know for sure that the bartender really saw Winston. He may have gotten Winston confused with someone else."

"You have jurisdiction, and I can help." Her wide eyes beseeched him. "Come on, Colt. If he's the one who shot at my house, it's only fair to allow me the opportunity to assist in finding him."

"What if this attack was the result of something else?" He wasn't entirely convinced the shooter was Blaine. "I'm sure there are other bad guys you've helped put away."

She shrugged. "None as dangerous as Blaine. Regardless, I'll have to leave that investigation to the detective who'll be assigned to the case. But you and I both know you're here in Jackson because Blaine was sighted in the area. And there is a possibility he came to exact his revenge."

He couldn't deny her comment. And he'd already considered asking for her help, as she knew Winston the best of anyone, but he wasn't sure his boss would approve.

If the shooter was Winston, there was always the possibility the guy would return to make another attempt to kill Morganne. The idea sent a cold chill down his spine.

She'd be safer with him. She might be a trained law enforcement officer, yet he didn't like the idea of Winston getting a hold of her for a second time.

In his opinion, the fact that she'd gotten away the first time was incredible.

"Yeah, okay," he relented. "But what about your job?"

"I'll take care of it. I think I can convince my boss to assign me to this case. Give me five minutes." Morganne spun around and ran back to her house.

Colt followed more slowly, knowing this was a bad idea yet unwilling to back down on his offer.

Apprehending a known serial killer before he harmed anyone else was the most important thing.

And if Morganne could help even in the smallest way, Colt refused to pass on the opportunity.

He only hoped he didn't live to regret it.

TWO

Morganne's five minutes turned out to be far longer. She chafed at the delay, as her fellow officers wanted her to help examine the footprints in her muddy backyard. While she did that, she accepted Colt's offer to board up her shattered bedroom window.

She understood and appreciated her colleagues' desire to find the person responsible for shooting at her. Any attack on a cop was taken seriously. And despite her gender, and the teasing she often put up with, when an officer of the law became a target, all brothers and sisters in blue bonded together to protect the cop family.

After switching the breaker switch back on, she went outside to activate the lights.

When she crouched down, it was easy to find and eliminate her prints.

"This here—" She pointed at the one with the toe of the boot pointed toward the woods. "Looks fresh and isn't mine or Marshal Nelson's."

"Are you sure?" Officer Jamison asked.

"Yes. I don't know if you noticed, but Marshal Nelson is wearing cowboy boots. This print here has the rounded toe and tread of a hiking boot." She gazed down at it thoughtfully.

Five years ago, Blaine Winston had chosen his victims carefully. One victim was found on a running trail; another time, he'd chosen a victim in a state park, and the very last victim had been found off one of the well-known hiking trails.

The hiking-boot print wasn't proof the shooter was Winston, but it made her chest tighten, all the same. His attack on her had been late at night after she finished a shift at the local restaurant, and she still remembered the stark terror at being grabbed from behind.

And to this day, she was thankful that her father had forced her to learn self-defense and martial arts, enabling her to fight with enough force to escape.

Morganne's mother had died when she was eight in a car crash, and for years it had been just her and her dad. She'd been bullied as a kid, so her dad taught her everything he knew about guns and self-defense so she could protect herself.

Her skills had been put to the test when Blaine had attacked her.

Afterward, she'd become a cop. Her dad hadn't loved the idea, but when she'd passed the academy with flying colors, he became her biggest supporter. Until Pop had passed away from a sudden heart attack last year.

She'd been thankful her father had died before Blaine had escaped. Her dad would have tried to protect her 24-7 if he'd known her cousin was out there somewhere.

"We'll measure and photograph this print, to record it as evidence," Jamison said, bringing her back to the present.

"What did you find?" Colt joined them in the brightly lit backyard.

"Hiking-boot print." She frowned up at Colt. "I'm still trying to understand why Blaine would come back here after eluding law enforcement for nine months. In that amount of time, he would have had to obtain a false identity, a vehicle and a gun."

"Yeah," Colt said, nodding. "I think it's clear he has help."

She paled. "Who would do that? I mean, sure, he had friends, but none that would want to be associated with a murderer." Blaine didn't really match the profile of a serial killer. He was a twenty-eight-year-old white male when he was arrested, but he wasn't a loner. In fact, he'd had plenty of friends and came across as gregarious, if rather annoying. It had been a shock to discover that his outgoing persona had hidden a monster within.

He hadn't displayed any of the charm associated with some serial killers, and no evidence of killing animals as a young child, either. At least, that she was aware of.

Colt drew her aside and lowered his voice. "I know it's been nine months, but do you have any information on who may have helped Winston escape? We know the ambulance crash must have been a setup. The same person who did that for him could be the one helping him now."

Morganne knew Colt's question was legitimate, but it still bothered her that everyone assumed she was intimately familiar with her cousin.

She wasn't, other than being the victim who had gotten away, but she probably knew more about his family history than anyone else. "Blaine's mother divorced his father when he was ten. They had joint custody until Blaine decided to live with his father full-time, and I got the impression Blaine and his mother didn't get along. But she's dead now. I doubt his father, Silas Winston, would help him, and I know the Feds talked to Silas several times after Blaine escaped. Still, it may be worth taking another shot at questioning Silas."

"I agree." Colt swept his gaze around the yard. "How much longer until we can get out of here?"

She understood his need to move forward sooner rather than later. But if there were more clues the shooter had left behind, it would behoove them to investigate.

"Let's just spend a few more minutes looking at the prints," Morganne suggested. "For all we know, his helper was here with him."

"Good point." The admiration in Colt's gaze was nice, but she told herself it didn't matter. He was probably like her colleagues who were constantly amazed when she held her own against criminals.

Including one dirty cop.

They fanned out to look for more evidence. Morganne found another hiking-boot print, but it was only a partial, not as good as the full. But the direction of the toes indicated the shooter had run this way to reach the road.

She belatedly realized her decision to shut the floodlights down so she could try to find the shooter may have had the opposite effect of helping him escape.

"Morganne?" Colt's voice interrupted her depressing thoughts. "Come take a look."

She joined him at the edge of her woods. Crouching down, she saw a tuft of fabric on a thorn. "Could have been left by anyone, including me."

"Except there's another partial print right here, too." Colt backed off so she could see the area he was talking about. Sure enough, another hiking-boot heel print could be seen near the bush.

She rose to her feet and turned to face her house. There was a direct line of sight from here to her bedroom window. "This could be where he was standing when he took the shot," she murmured.

"My thoughts exactly. Let's see if we can find the shell casing to test our theory."

They both crouched down and carefully scanned the debris-laden ground. Morganne moved to the side so the floodlights could better illuminate the area.

She lifted the branches of a low shrub and smiled with satisfaction. "Found it."

"Looks like a thirty aught six, or something along those lines," Colt said thoughtfully. He turned and looked at the distance between this location and her house. "Seventy-five yards, give or take."

"Seventy-two, according to the property boundaries outlined on the purchase agreement." She glanced over her shoulder. "Jamison? We found more evidence, including the shell casing."

"Good eye," Jamison said as he approached.

"Marshal Nelson found the fabric first, and the partial print." She gave credit where it was due. "Mark it for now, and get the crime scene techs to take photos first before bagging the evidence."

"I can do that." Jamison stuck a flag in the soft earth.

Morganne glanced at Colt. They could poke around in the woods, but she didn't think they'd gain much. "If the shooter had help, could be the assistant stayed in the car, which is how they escaped so quickly."

Colt nodded. "Do you want to continue searching here?"

"No." They hadn't found any footprints other than the hiking shoe, Colt's cowboy boots and her running shoes. "Let's go."

Colt nodded and followed her to the house. She'd taken a few minutes to throw a change of clothes and toiletries in a duffel bag. She grabbed the strap, intending to sling it over her shoulder, but Colt stopped her.

"I'll take that for you."

Morganne knew he was just being polite, but she doubted he'd do that for another marshal. "I can manage."

He tipped his head to the side. "I know you can manage—you're a strong woman, and a cop. But I was always taught to carry a woman's bags."

She fought the impulse to be treated as an equal but decided there was no point in complaining. Colt was only trying to be nice. After handing him the bag, she followed him outside. "Where are you parked?"

"Four houses down, around the curve in the road." He glanced at her. "Do you think heading to Silas Winston's place is worth our time? It may be better to stick around in Jackson since this was where Blaine was last sighted." Colt paused then added, "If the bartender really recognized him."

She considered his question carefully. "Yes. Silas lives in Rock Springs, which is roughly three hours from here. At the very least, we need to rule Silas out as Blaine's accomplice."

"Okay, sounds like a plan." Colt opened her car door for her, then tossed her duffel into the back. "I'm hungry, so we'll stop and grab breakfast to go along the way."

She nodded and sat back against the seat. "Coffee would be nice."

"Do you have any other ideas on where we can find Winston?"

She shook her head. "If he's not staying with Silas, then we need to consider he may be hiding out in a motel."

Colt shook his head. "That would be risky, as his mug shot has been plastered all over the news. Only an idiot would give him a motel room."

"But if he has fake ID, and altered his appearance even a little, the motel clerks may not look past the nose on their face."

"True, although still risky."

"So was going to a tavern," she pointed out. "Although he could also be hiding in an abandoned house."

"There are plenty of those around." Colt pulled into the drive-through lane of a fast-food restaurant.

She tried not to look dejected. "Far too many possibilities, especially if you consider the number of ghost towns around the area." There were a lot of old mining towns that had closed down once the mines were stripped. "Narrowing down his hiding place won't be easy."

"I know." Colt turned his attention to the drive-through speaker. She raised a brow as Colt ordered a full breakfast meal—sandwich, hash brown potatoes and a large coffee. He waved his hand, indicating she should place her order.

She requested an egg sandwich and large coffee. When she tried to pay her share, he shook his head.

"I've got it. You're the one helping me out."

"Colt, you need to treat me as an equal partner in this."

He opened his mouth, then seemed to

change his mind about what he was about to say. "You're right. We'll split the expenses from here on."

"Good." Morganne would be using her savings to pay her share, but that was okay. Her boss hadn't been thrilled with her request to work the case as a special assignment, but he'd ultimately agreed since she was one of Blaine's victims, and the one to help bring him to justice five years ago.

She only hoped she could repeat that same success a second time around.

When she finished her sandwich, she sipped her coffee, thinking about her uncle Silas. "Do you think the locals are watching Silas's house in case Blaine shows up?"

"I don't know, but probably not after all this time." He glanced at her. "I was in Idaho Falls when I got news of the sighting in Jackson. As far as I'm aware, this is the first sighting of the guy since he dropped off the face of the earth after his escape nine months ago."

"What's in Idaho Falls?"

"Another case. Not pertaining to this one. My boss pulled me off that protection detail to track Winston."

"There has to be more than one US marshal trying to find the guy," she protested. "Shouldn't they have choppers up sweeping the area?"

"Not based on one unverified sighting." He shrugged. "Local law enforcement agencies across several states were put on alert back when he initially escaped, and you know how it is. It's difficult to sustain that level of vigilance for long. Certainly not for nine months. That's why I was sent here first, to verify that the guy the bartender saw really was Winston. Once that has been confirmed, we should be able to pull in more resources."

"I guess that makes sense." There was a lot of wide-open space in Wyoming, and truthfully, Blaine could be hiding anywhere. Especially if he had help from an accomplice.

Silas? Maybe. Who else? She honestly

didn't know. Maybe a former cellmate, someone who had gotten out of prison in the five years since Blaine had been convicted? Or someone he knew prior to his arrest?

She sat back, watching as Colt's SUV ate up the miles. He was speeding, but she didn't mind. The sooner they reached Silas's place, the better.

Morganne stared out the passenger-side window, hoping they'd get a lead on Blaine's whereabouts very soon.

Before he killed again.

Colt finished the last of his coffee, sensing Morganne's grim mood.

He'd gotten his boss to send him Silas's DMV information, learning the guy had an old brown Chevy Impala registered in his name. Morganne had remembered him having the vehicle from the last time she'd seen him. They'd made good time, coming into Rock Springs in two hours instead of the usual three. He pulled into a gas station and glanced at her. "Bathroom breaks and fuel before we head over to Silas Winston's place."

"Okay." She slid out of the SUV and headed inside.

He'd gotten gas in Jackson, but he wanted to be prepared in case they got a hot lead on Winston's whereabouts. He wasn't sure if the local police had been to Silas's house in the hours since Blaine had allegedly been sighted in Jackson, but even if they had, he wanted to see the place for himself.

Ten minutes later they were back on the road. "He lives on the outskirts of town," Morganne informed him.

He followed her directions until they came upon a trailer home, missing several slats of siding. From the side angle, he could see the backyard was fenced in, which made him worry that Winston could be hiding out back there. He pulled off to the side of the road several yards away and turned toward Morganne.

"How do you want to approach it?"

"You should go up and knock at the front door. I'll sneak around back."

He frowned. "I don't like that plan."

She huffed. "Then why did you ask for my opinion?"

It wasn't that he was chauvinistic—he truly admired Morganne's skills. But he didn't like the thought of her being in danger. He told himself to trust that God would protect her. "Okay, okay."

"I know the place better than you do. There's a small shed in the backyard. I'll want to clear that first before you try the front door."

He pulled the brim of his hat down and blew out a breath. She'd asked to be treated as a partner, so that's what he'd do. He pulled out his phone. "Fine. We need to exchange numbers so you can text me when you want me to approach from the front."

She rattled off her cell phone number. He punched in the information, then called her so she'd have his.

"I'll text you." She jumped from the SUV, pulled her service weapon and ran alongside the fence toward the back of the trailer.

Colt watched her disappear from view. He tapped his fingers on the steering wheel, striving for patience. Morganne might be a beautiful woman, but she was also a well-trained cop.

No reason to be nervous. Hadn't she already proved herself capable by escaping Blaine's attack five years ago? And again, when she'd helped rescue Duncan and Chelsey last year? Not to mention she did know more about the property than he did.

Still, his usual patience and faith had abandoned him. His tension was wound tighter than a piano wire.

As he was about to push out of the car to check on her, his phone vibrated. With relief, he read the text.

Backyard clear. Go.

He eased from the SUV and approached the trailer house from the front. Based on the fact that Morganne didn't find anything in the back, he wasn't expecting anyone to answer his knock.

After rapping sharply on the door twice, he tested the knob. It wasn't locked. Shooting a quick glance over his shoulder, he opened the door and eased in.

The place was dusty, the air ripe with the odors of sour milk, alcohol and unwashed dishes. He quickly cleared the living room and kitchen areas, then went down the narrow hall to the bathroom and two small bedrooms.

He'd just finished when Morganne joined him. "How did you get in?" she asked.

"The front door wasn't locked," he confirmed. "How about you?"

"Picked the back door lock. Unfortunately, I'm out of practice, so it took me longer than usual."

Her wry comment made him smile. "Well, it looks to me like Silas left in a hurry," Colt said. "There's no sign of his Impala, either."

She turned and went back to the main living space. She wrinkled her nose. "He's been gone for a while, twenty-four hours at least."

"Think he's with Blaine?" Colt came up to stand beside her. "I mean, it would make sense that his father would help him escape."

"Maybe." She gestured toward the mess in the kitchen. "No obvious signs of a struggle."

He concurred. "So it's a dead end."

Morganne didn't answer, taking her time going through the place. She went into the kitchen and looked around carefully.

He reined in his impatience. Now that they knew Blaine, and Silas for that matter, weren't here, he was anxious to move on.

"Colt?" Morganne called.

His pulse spiked as he hurried to join her in the kitchen. "What's wrong?"

She looked down at a small red spot on

the edge of the sink. "Doesn't this look like blood?"

He frowned. "Yeah, it does. But one small spot of blood doesn't mean Silas was the victim of a crime. Maybe he cut himself shaving?"

"Silas hasn't shaved in years." Morganne went down on her haunches and pointed at another area. "Here's another spot. And another."

He could see now that she had found a very small trail of blood spots that in his opinion looked relatively fresh. "You think we should get some crime scene techs out here? Match the blood with the DNA they have on file for Blaine?"

"Yes, absolutely. But finding this raises a bigger concern."

"Like what?" He wasn't following her train of thought.

She rose to her feet. "Let's say this blood matches Silas. Did Blaine come here to force his father to help him? If so, why do that when he already had help from whoever hit the ambulance, helping him to escape in the first place?"

It was a good point. He glanced back down at the blood. "It's not much to go on."

"Maybe, but I saw this, too." She led the way into the bedroom and pointed at a silver belt buckle depicting a rodeo rider. "Silas wore this belt buckle every single day. His favorite stories were about his days riding bucking broncos in the local rodeo. He made a lot of money as a young man, which is how he convinced my dad's sister to marry him." She shook her head. "Blaine followed in his footsteps, also working the rodeo circuit, but he didn't have nearly as much talent as my uncle. Either way, I can't see Silas leaving it behind like this. Not when it was one of his prized possessions."

"Your theory is Blaine showed up here unannounced and forced Silas into helping him?" That was a lot of assumption to place on a belt buckle.

She snapped her fingers and whirled away. Curious, he followed her into the fenced-in backyard. Morganne headed straight for the small shed and yanked the door open.

"I thought you already cleared it?" he asked.

"I peeked in long enough to confirm Blaine wasn't hiding out here. But I remembered seeing something dark on the ground." She pulled out her phone and used the flashlight app to illuminate the area.

He whistled softly. "More blood, and it's still wet, so it hasn't been here long."

"Yeah." Morganne's gaze was grim. "This makes me think Blaine was here, and he forced Silas to help him. We need to alert the state police to be on the lookout for his Chevy."

Colt nodded, hoping Winston hadn't added another murder to his scorecard.

THREE

Morganne suppressed a shiver. This wasn't the first crime scene she'd been to, or even the worst one.

Yet it hit hard, because this one was personal.

She hadn't been close to her uncle Silas. The guy spent too much time at bars and was an angry drunk. Her aunt Marge had divorced Silas when Morganne had only been four years old, so she didn't have many clear memories of the time when they were together. Marge and Silas had agreed to a joint custody arrangement until Blaine was thirteen, when he had declared his desire to live with his father full-time.

No matter Silas's faults, he didn't deserve to be injured by his own son.

Or physically forced into hiding him.

The blood wasn't a good sign. She rose and headed back out into the fresh air. The sun had come up during their drive from Jackson to Rock Springs, and she welcomed the warmth on her face, even though the early May breeze was cool.

She absently fingered the small scar along the side of her neck. After five years, it had faded to the point it was barely visible to the human eye, but she could still feel the burn of the rope. Feel Blaine's hot breath on the back of her neck.

Hear his guttural voice as he told her he was going to kill her.

She still sometimes wondered how she'd escaped. Yes, she'd learned self-defense and martial arts because of the kids at school bullying her. Yet Blaine had had the rope around her neck in a heartbeat and had arm strength from rodeo riding on his side.

Maybe he'd simply underestimated how much she'd fight back.

To this day, she couldn't be sure Blaine had known who she was the night he'd attacked. She felt certain he must have recognized her, but it had been dark, clouds obliterating the moon, and she'd worn her hair back in a bun to keep it out of her face while she'd worked at the restaurant. He'd attacked her from behind, so he wouldn't have gotten a good look at her face.

Unless, of course, he'd planned his attack well ahead of time. Targeting her on purpose specifically because of the DNA they shared.

"Morganne? Are you okay?"

She snapped back to the present, dropping her hand from her neck. "Yes, of course. I'm trying to figure out where to go next."

"We could head back to Jackson," Colt offered. "I still need to talk to the bartender who claimed to have seen Winston last night."

Talking to the bartender directly was the right thing to do, but she'd rather stay on Blaine's trail if possible. "How fresh is this blood? Do you think Blaine came here first before heading to Jackson?"

Colt stepped back inside the storage shed to look closely at the blood soaked into the dirt floor. "I'm no expert, but to me, this looks as if it may have happened yesterday rather than this morning." He glanced up at her. "We were only about an hour behind him leaving your place, and we made up time on the interstate to get here. Even if he risked speeding, which I doubt, as more than one criminal has been brought to justice by committing a minor traffic violation, I don't think Blaine would have had enough time to get here and coerce Silas into helping him before we arrived."

He made a good point, and she couldn't help feeling dejected. "We're back to square one, Colt. I honestly have no idea where Blaine is now."

"We'll find him." Colt spoke with a confidence she wished she shared. He left the shed to stand beside her. "Do you think the sighting at the Wagon Wheel Tavern is legit? That Winston had the audacity to go into a public place?"

"Silas likes to drink. You may have noticed the empty liquor bottles in the kitchen among the mess. Could be Blaine made the stop at the bar in an effort to appease his father. You know, 'thanks for the help, Pop, even though I had to hurt you to get you to cooperate.'"

"That's a fair point. And that settles it." Colt strode toward the fence gateway. "We'll call the locals to work this crime scene and pray the state police find the Impala. In the meantime, we'll return to Jackson to talk to the bartender. Maybe he noticed a second man but didn't think they were together for some reason."

"Can't hurt." Unfortunately, she couldn't come up with a better plan. It seemed risky for Blaine to have gone to the Wagon Wheel, but maybe his arrogance at having escaped without a trace for the past nine months made him feel invincible.

But not for long, she silently promised. She planned to do whatever was necessary to ensure Blaine Winston went back to jail where he belonged.

As they returned to Colt's SUV, she glanced at her watch. "This is when a plane would come in handy. Two hours to drive here to Jackson, only to turn around and drive at least another two hours back. It's a big waste of time."

Colt nodded. "I understand your concern, but unless we can verify Winston is still in the area, my boss isn't going to approve the expense of a chopper or a fixed-wing plane."

She scowled. "What about the blood at Silas's place? Isn't that evidence we can use for additional resources?"

He slanted her a glance. "Not unless we find Blaine's blood. Your uncle could have had an altercation with anyone over anything."

Colt was right and she knew it. But it still grated on her nerves to be hampered by the distance between cities in the vast Wyoming countryside.

A fact that obviously worked to Blaine's advantage.

"Who were Blaine's friends?" Colt asked when they were back on the interstate heading to Jackson. "Where did he hang out prior to his arrest?"

"He hung out with a group of guys that were part of the rodeo circuit." She struggled to remember names. "I believe Vince Lange and Owen Plumber were friends of his. Owen showed up in the courtroom at Blaine's arraignment, but not Vince. I was surprised, as they had both been tight with Blaine. I think Vince distanced himself after he learned of the evidence against Blaine, some of which I was able to provide." She curled her fingers into fists, remembering how she'd gotten Blaine's DNA beneath her nails as she'd fought him off.

"Okay, those are good names to start

with." A note of excitement lifted his tone. "It's possible Blaine reached out to them."

"Maybe, but if he contacted them, you'd think they would have gone to the police." That's what any good citizen would do.

"Not if they still felt some sort of loyalty toward him." He glanced at her. "I remember reading that Blaine's initial statement was that he thought you were his girlfriend and simply wanted to surprise you. He claimed the rope was a joke."

She scoffed. "Some joke. Good thing no one believed him. Especially since his DNA was found on the other three victims." The DNA results had taken almost two full months to return, but they came back as a match. It had given her a strong sense of satisfaction at being the one to bring Blaine Winston to justice. "Once his lawyer found out about the results, he convinced Blaine to plead guilty."

Colt surprised her by reaching over to clasp her hand lightly. "I'm glad you didn't have to testify against him, Morganne."

"Me, too." She gently squeezed his hand back. "Blaine knew he was facing a losing battle. Juries love DNA evidence, and my testimony would have been the final nail in his coffin."

"Yeah, no doubt."

At the time, it had been a huge relief not to testify. She'd suffered nightmares after the attack, always waking up just as she feared she would die of asphyxiation. Then she'd learned of the intercepted letters Blaine had sent, threatening notes that had been a weak attempt to intimidate her. Counseling helped, but the best thing she'd done to put the past behind her once and for all was to take and pass the police academy exam.

She'd vowed never to be a victim again, and more, to support those who were by doing her part to bring the bad guys to justice.

A promise she reaffirmed now. She and Colt would find Blaine and send him back to jail.

Morganne swallowed hard, unable to bear the thought that Blaine might escape for good. Disappearing under a different name, seeking refuge in another country. Free to continue his murdering ways.

Colt pushed the speed limit in his haste to return to Jackson. He considered asking his boss, James Crane, for a chopper and plane, as Morganne suggested, but he knew it would be a waste of time.

He'd hold off until they had a good lead to work with. Then his boss would have a better reason to call in the cavalry.

"Blaine had a girlfriend at the time of his arrest," Morganne said in a thoughtful tone. "I remember she was horrified by what he'd done. Her name was Kay Fisher." She turned a bit in her seat to face him. "You don't think Blaine would seek revenge against her, too, do you?"

His gut tensed, and he hoped they hadn't missed something important. "I'm not aware of him sending any threatening notes to her. And she didn't do anything that assisted in his arrest. Not the way you did."

"I know." She grimaced and pulled out her phone. "Still, I'm going to find her most recent address. It can't hurt to warn her."

The idea that Winston had come back to Jackson to tie up all loose ends was disturbing. Had Blaine's father, Silas, been one of those loose ends? Was that why they'd found blood in the guy's shed? Maybe Blaine hadn't wanted Silas to help but had chosen to kill him instead?

But if Silas wasn't his accomplice, then who was? No way could Blaine pull this off on his own. Colt felt certain the guy had help.

Colt instinctively slowed his speed in case they needed to turn around to go back to Rock Springs.

"Jamison? Kimball here. I need you to do a DMV run for me on a woman by the name of Kay Fisher." Morganne spelled out the full name for him. "I need a recent address for her."

There was nothing but silence for a long moment, before Morganne said, "Jackson? Are you sure?"

That news was enough for Colt to hit the gas, increasing their speed. He was glad to know Blaine's former girlfriend lived in Jackson, since it made returning to the city worth their time.

Not that he expected Kay Fisher to provide any leads as to Blaine's current whereabouts. But she absolutely deserved to know about the reported sighting of the guy.

As they approached the Jackson city limits, he saw Morganne glancing down at her phone. "Did he send you Fisher's address?"

"Yes, it's on the other side of town from where I live." She flashed a wry smile. "Let's drive past the Wagon Wheel first and check the place out. It's still early, so if they don't have anyone for us to talk to, we'll head over to Kay's house."

"Good plan." He was forced to slow his speed as he headed into town. The Wagon Wheel was also on the opposite side of town, so that was helpful.

The Wagon Wheel was a typical country-western bar. In the bright light of the morning, it looked worn and uninviting. But Colt knew that by early afternoon, the country music would be blaring and patrons would gather, ready to enjoy food and drink.

Especially today, on a Friday.

Would Blaine and his father return tonight? Doubtful. If anything, they'd choose another spot, if they decided to stay in the area at all.

Colt still couldn't understand why Blaine would bother to return. Nine long months, with no hint of where he'd been hiding. He should have been basking in the Mexican sun or bundled up in the cold Canadian mountains.

Hopefully, this wasn't a wild-goose chase. Although the blood at Silas's trailer gave him hope they were on the right track.

Colt parked his SUV in the empty lot and slid out from behind the wheel. He stretched and tried to ignore the rumbling of his stomach. It had only been four hours since they'd eaten their fast-food breakfast, but he was already trying to decide where to have lunch.

He knew his buddies made fun of his obsession with food. What he'd never told them was that he grew up dirt poor, often not knowing when his next meal would be.

Or even if there would be any food in his house at all.

Things had been rough during his high school years. If not for his girlfriend Abby, he would have headed down a bad path. He'd managed to get a scholarship to college, and they'd planned on getting married after graduation. Only that hadn't happened.

Losing Abby six years ago in a carjacking had been devastating, and only through God's will had he gotten through it. He'd joined the US Marshals afterward, knowing the job would take him to many different locations across a wide territory. It was a role that suited him just fine, because his heart would always belong to his high school sweetheart.

"Looks like they don't open until eleven," Morganne said, interrupting his trip down memory lane. Together they crossed to the tavern. "It's only ten fifteen."

"I'm hoping a manager might be in early to set things up for the day." He tried the door. It was locked, so he banged his fist on it. "This is US federal marshal Colt Nelson. I need to talk to you."

He heard movement from inside, then the lock clicked and the door opened. A grizzled guy who could have been anywhere between forty and seventy years of age peered out. "Whaddya want?"

"I'd like to speak to Neal Henderson, the

bartender who was working last night." Colt flashed his creds so the guy could see he was a marshal. "And I'd also like to speak to the owner. Is that you, sir?"

The grizzled man stared at him for several long moments before shifting his gaze to include Morganne. "I'm Cully White, the owner. Come on in."

"Thanks, Mr. White." Colt held the door for Morganne as they headed inside to the grim interior of the tavern. Like the outside, the interior also looked worn in the early-morning light.

"Just call me Cully. Everyone does." Cully squinted at them. "Neal isn't here. He closed the place at two in the morning and won't be back until three thirty to work his happy hour shift."

"Do you know Silas Winston?" Colt asked, knowing it wasn't likely since the guy lived in Rock Springs.

"Nah. But I heard that Blaine Winston was apparently spotted here last evening. Neal called to warn me the cops would be sniffing around." Cully crossed his arms over his broad chest. "All my licenses are up-to-date."

"I don't care about your liquor license," Colt assured him. "But I would like to talk to Neal Henderson and anyone else who may have seen Blaine Winston."

Cully's gaze narrowed. "You askin' for the names of my patrons? Not sure I like that."

"Please, Cully." Morganne smiled at the old guy. "I almost died when Blaine Winston attacked me five years ago. I'm worried he's come back to finish the job."

Cully's features softened, and he reluctantly nodded. "Okay, fine. I can give you information from those who used debit or credit cards, but I won't have a record of those who paid in cash."

"We'll take what we can get, thank you." As Cully White turned away, Colt shot Morganne a look of admiration. "Nicely done."

She grinned. "Most men out here aim to

protect their women. Besides, if the gunshot at my place was from Blaine, I didn't lie about his wanting to finish the job."

His smile faded. "I know."

Cully returned a few minutes later with a handful of receipts. "I made copies for my files—you can keep these."

"Thanks again, Cully." Colt took the pile of receipts from Cully's outstretched hands. "Would you also be willing to give us Neal Henderson's address and phone number?"

"I reckon I can do that," Cully said slowly. "But it's still early. He probably didn't leave here until close to three in the morning, since it takes a while to clean the place up after closing. You should wait until later to try talking to him."

"Of course, we'll wait for a while," Morganne assured him. "We won't interfere with Neal's ability to work his shift."

"Good." Cully gave a curt nod. "Friday nights are the busiest for us, sometimes better than Saturdays. Lots of folks like starting their weekend with a little fun."

Fun was relative. Personally Colt wouldn't want to spend his time in a crowded place like this, but he simply nodded. "We won't wake him up too early," he promised.

Cully left again, returning with a scrap of paper. The owner handed it to Morganne, who thanked him.

They walked out into the bright May sunshine. He followed Morganne to the SUV. "Let's talk to Kay Fisher, then find someplace to eat. We can use that time to sketch out a plan for the rest of the day."

"Lunch? Already?" She glanced at him over her shoulder. "It's kind of early."

At that moment, he noticed a flash of something off in the trees. Sunlight bouncing off a rifle scope?

"Get down!" He leaped forward and jerked Morganne's arm, yanking her off her feet at the exact same moment gunfire echoed around them.

"What in the world?" Morganne gasped.

"Shooter is straight ahead. Get behind the SUV." He practically dragged her with him to the shelter of the vehicle. He pulled out his phone and dialed 911 to report the gunfire.

"If that's Blaine, we need to go after him," Morganne said in a low voice.

"Not when he has a rifle with a scope. Too easy for him to pick us off."

"We can't just sit here," Morganne protested. "We have to do something."

He understood and shared her need to find the shooter. But not while they were sitting ducks. If the shooter was Blaine, the guy had gone on the attack.

The hunter had just become the hunted.

FOUR

Morganne stared at Colt, trying not to show her impatience. They needed to move, *now*. "Let's split up, the same way we did at my place. We need to find and arrest Blaine."

Colt's expression was grim, but he nodded slowly. "Okay, although it's possible the shooter isn't Winston. But we need to know for sure, so let's do this."

She didn't give him a second to change his mind. She ran in a crouch to the edge of the SUV, raking her gaze over the area. Good thing about being here in Jackson was that she knew the area very well.

Better, she hoped, than Blaine did. Because she knew in her gut he was the shooter. No way was this a coincidence.

There was a tree located about thirty yards away. Without hesitation, she rose and ran toward the bit of cover, expecting to hear more gunfire ringing out.

Nothing happened.

Had Blaine already gotten away? The possibility of losing him steeled her resolve. She huddled behind the tree, picking out her next location, then made another run for it. She hoped Colt was making similar progress. If they did this right, they should be able to box Blaine in.

She pinpointed another location and ran. Her foot slipped on a rock, and she stumbled just as another shot rang out, missing her by inches. Her pulse spiked. She dived to the ground, rolled and took cover behind some brush.

There was another gunshot, but not from a rifle, likely from Colt's handgun. He was shooting to draw Blaine's fire.

Leaping up, she ran again, sweeping her gaze over the wooded area for Blaine's hiding spot. She heard noises, then the rumble of a car engine.

No! Not again! With every ounce of strength she possessed, she ran through the woods, branches slapping her in the face, tugging on her hair and clothing, until she reached the opposite side and found a dirt road.

Dust particles still floated in the air, drifting to the ground, but the vehicle was gone. Was Blaine still using the same boxy vehicle she'd glimpsed earlier that morning? Maybe.

Colt joined her, his expression tense as his keen eye searched for signs of injury.

"We lost him." Morganne couldn't hide her dismay. "So close, yet he still managed to get away."

"Better to lose him than you," Colt said tersely.

She frowned, then understood what he'd meant. "Yeah, I guess that second shot was meant for me."

"You're clearly his main target, Morganne." He looked up and down the dirt road. "He took a risk attempting to get to you in broad daylight."

"Maybe, but he's arrogant that way. And know this—he'll kill you, too, Colt." The grim realization sank deep. She was Blaine's target, but if Colt continued working with her, he'd become collateral damage. She swallowed hard. "Maybe I should continue on alone."

"Not happening." Colt's words were harsh. "We're in this together. Our partnership in searching for Winston provides our strongest ability to take him down."

There was truth to his statement. Two cops hunting Blaine down was better than one. Frankly, the more, the merrier.

But it didn't sit well to know that others could die because of Blaine's obsession with killing her.

Because she'd gotten away and helped arrest him for multiple murders? It was the only motive she could come up with.

"Let's see if we can find his brass or

other clues," Colt said, pulling her back to the present. "Would be nice to find a match to the shell casing we found in your backyard."

"Okay, but we need to check on his old girlfriend, too," she said with a frown. "I don't want to believe she's helping him, but he could have forced her into it by holding her at gunpoint. The same way he may have done with Silas."

Colt tipped his cowboy hat back and nodded. "Okay, we'll let the crime scene techs comb the area, instead."

Morganne made the call to her lieutenant, explaining to Graves what they needed.

"I already have officers headed to the Wagon Wheel," he confirmed. "I sent Jamison home. The guy has been up all night. Abrams should be there, though. And the crime scene tech will get there soon, too."

"Thanks, boss," Morganne said.

"We'll need your statement, Kimball, and the deputy marshal's as well."

She swallowed another flash of impatience. Her boss was a good guy, but there wasn't time to waste. "They'll be short statements, sir. Neither one of us saw the shooter. Right now, we need to head out to follow up on another lead. We'll check back in with you later."

"Kimball," Graves protested.

"Boss, we need to catch this guy ASAP." She could feel her patience slipping. "If there was something to tell you about the incident, I'd let you know. Try to trust me on this, okay?"

"Fine," he relented. "But I expect you to report in soon."

"Later." She disconnected and noticed Colt was peering down at the dirt road. "Did you find something?"

"Part of a tire tread." He took his phone and snapped a picture. "No guarantee it's from Winston's vehicle. Looks wider than a regular car tire, so it's not from your uncle's Impala."

Morganne nodded, because he was right to be cautious. They couldn't jump on every possible scrap of evidence without something to back it up. She pulled out her own phone. "Share the pic with me, would you? If we find his vehicle, this could help."

Colt sent her the photo, then led the way through the woods back to where they'd left his SUV.

It was impossible to ignore the sense of urgency. They needed to figure out what Blaine's next move might be.

Well, other than his trying to kill her.

Although, the more she thought about that, the more she considered using herself as bait to draw her cousin out of hiding.

No one would like her plan, least of all Colt. But that didn't matter—not compared to succeeding in their mission to get Blaine back into police custody.

As they emerged from the woods, they

were met by several Jackson police officers. She crossed over to Abrams. "Just spoke to the lieutenant. He agreed we can provide statements later. We need to get back to tracking this guy."

Abrams looked annoyed but didn't argue. "Fine, but I'll need those statements to finish my report."

"I'm aware." Paperwork was the bane of every cop's existence. "We'll provide them as soon as possible."

"Fine, go." Abrams waved his hand.

She glanced at Colt, and they headed over to his SUV. One of the squad cars had blocked him in, so they had to wait for the officer to move it before they could get out. Glancing back over her shoulder, she winced when she saw Cully White standing outside his front door, waving his arms at the officers. The grizzled old man looked like he might have a heart attack over the possible negative impact to his business.

She felt guilty, but it wasn't her fault

Blaine had found them at the Wagon Wheel. And how had he done that, anyway?

"You're sure we weren't followed from Rock Springs?"

"I've been watching for a tail and haven't seen anyone lingering behind us. But can I tell you with absolute certainty we weren't?" Colt shrugged and shook his head. "Nothing is impossible. Especially if Winston has a high-powered scope on that rifle of his. There are only so many highways between cities out here. He could have easily found a place to hide, wait and watch for the opportunity to take a shot at us."

"Not that many places, and the terrain is relatively flat, especially between those ghost towns." She frowned. "However, he could have been on the outskirts of Jackson, waiting for us to return."

"My thought exactly."

She let out a heavy sigh. "It's making me mad how he's one step ahead of us.

As law enforcement officers, it should be the other way around."

"That would be true if he was trying to get away from us," Colt argued. "But he's not. Instead of leaving Wyoming, he's sticking around to kill you."

It wasn't anything she hadn't already told herself, yet hearing Colt's blunt statement made her shiver. She wanted nothing more than to draw Blaine out of hiding, but she wasn't ready to die, either.

She appreciated Colt's concern. As a cop she accepted being in danger. That was very different from knowing someone personally wanted to hunt you down and kill you.

She thought briefly of how her mother had sought solace in church. A habit she and her father hadn't continued after her death.

Was it too late?

"I need directions to Kay Fisher's house," Colt reminded her.

Glancing at his handsome profile, she

nodded and gestured with her hand. "Turn right at the next light."

"Gotcha," he drawled.

She told herself to stay focused on the case. She needed to stay sharp, allowing nothing to distract her. Especially not memories of her parents, or even the handsome marshal at her side.

The only way to capture Blaine was to beat him at his own deadly game.

Colt had never been more aware of a woman, and he didn't like it one bit. He'd loved Abby, so why was he feeling so protective about Morganne? Because she was a fellow cop? Because she was a woman who'd been strong enough to escape a killer like Winston?

He couldn't explain the strange phenomenon and did his best to shake it off. Most of his partners had been guys, Slade and Tanner in particular. Must be that he'd gotten into a bit of a rut working with them. He couldn't let Morganne mess with his head.

"Take a right at the next intersection," Morganne said. "I'm thinking we may want to approach her place with caution."

He sent a sidelong glance. "Good point. We were ambushed once at the Wagon Wheel. And once before that if you consider he staked out your house and tried to shoot you through the window." Thinking about the two near misses in a short time frame was sobering. He sent up a silent prayer of thanks to God for watching over them before adding, "If Winston's ex-girlfriend is helping him, voluntarily or not, he could be waiting for us."

"Yeah." Morganne looked around then gestured with her hand. "Why don't you pull over into that gas station up ahead? It's a safe place to leave your SUV." She offered a wan smile. "We'll have to head the rest of the way on foot."

"Sounds like a plan." One that would

be better executed in darkness, but that wasn't an option.

Besides, the darkness would only benefit Winston, too.

"Do you have a pair of binoculars?"

"In the glove box."

Morganne found the binocs and grinned. "These will come in handy."

"I hope so." He found a place to park along the back of the convenience store building. Morganne came around to stand beside him. She gave him the binoculars and pulled out her phone.

"Okay, according to my phone map, Fisher lives at the end of a dead-end road." She held the device so he could see the spot she indicated. "It's best if we approach from the back, see if anything looks amiss."

"Okay, give me a sec." He took a moment to set the small alarm beneath the edge of his driver's-side door, then straightened. Morganne was still frowning down at her phone.

"Ready? Let's do it." He waved her forward, preferring to cover her back. Although considering Winston's recent attacks, anything was possible. Thankfully, Morganne knew the city better than he did, so it made sense to follow her lead.

Morganne led him down a street, then cut through the yards between a couple of houses before crouching beside a large pine tree. This side of town was closer to the mountains, and the majestic sight never failed to steal his breath. He dropped beside her and lifted the binocs, trying to figure out which of the homes was their target.

"Which one is it?" he asked in a low voice.

"See the house with pale blue siding?" It took a minute for him to pinpoint the place with the glasses.

"Yeah, I see it."

"According to the map app on my phone, that's where Kay lives. Do you see anyone nearby?"

"Give me a few minutes." He took his time scoping the place out, checking the roofs of nearby dwellings, then moving on to verify no one was up in a nearby tree. He felt certain that based on the trajectory of the shot that had gone over their heads when he'd pulled Morganne down, Winston had been perched in a tree behind the Wagon Wheel.

He wasn't going to make the same mistake again.

"Well?" Morganne whispered impatiently.

"I don't see any evidence that Winston has staked the place out," he admitted. "But give me more time. There are too many hiding spots for my peace of mind."

She sighed but didn't protest any further.

Colt wasn't going to take any shortcuts here. He moved his binoculars from one potential hiding spot to another, making sure the area was clear.

Then he repeated the sweep for a second time.

"Come on, Colt. We can't sit here forever."

He finally lowered the glasses. "I don't see anyone hiding from above."

"Okay, time to move in closer, then." Morganne rose to her feet. "Ready?"

"Yep." He rested his hand on his weapon. At this point, Kay Fisher was only a person of interest. The woman was most likely innocent of any wrongdoing. From the information he'd received from James Crane, the only threatening letters Winston had sent were to Morganne. Kay Fisher was never mentioned and hadn't been asked to testify against him at trial. A trial that hadn't been needed.

Then again, he couldn't be sure that Winston's defense lawyer hadn't asked her to be a character witness for him. If that was the case, had Fisher agreed? Or refused to have anything to do with the guy?

If the former, it was possible she did help him escape. Or at least help him get around town. If it was the latter,

Colt could see Winston seeking revenge against her, too.

Until they knew one way or the other, he planned to be on high alert.

Morganne ran forward, stopping near a slender tree. She frowned as she stared at the house. "Looks quiet—maybe she's not home?"

"We need to get closer, see if we can look through one of the windows." He glanced over his shoulder. "While hoping the neighbors don't call the cops."

The corner of Morganne's mouth lifted in a grin. "We are the police."

"Not in uniform," he pointed out.

She shrugged. "Lots of people around here know me pretty well. I'll tell them I'm on a special assignment. We'll be fine."

He watched as she ran up to the house and peered through a window. He quickly joined her, verifying for himself that there was no one in the living room.

"I'm going to head to the front, see if her car is in the driveway."

"Do you know what she drives?"

She frowned. "I didn't ask for the make and model, just her address, but we can easily obtain that information."

It would be good information to have, but it could wait until they were finished here. "Later, then. I'll follow you around to the front."

She didn't hesitate but moved alongside the house until she could peer around the corner. "No car in the driveway, but the garage door is closed."

"Give me a minute to look through the garage window." He moved without waiting, going around to the opposite side of the house. Glancing through the small square window, he noted it was empty.

Relaxing his guard just a bit, he quickly returned to Morganne. "No car in the garage. She's probably not home."

"Probably not, but let's try knocking." Morganne went up to the front door and knocked hard. "Ms. Fisher? This is Officer Kimball. Are you home?"

There was no answer.

She knocked again, then rang the bell. Still no response.

For all their precautions, it seemed as if this was a dead end. Unless… A horrible thought hit him.

What if Winston had taken Fisher hostage? He remembered the boxy vehicle that had left the shooting scene at Morganne's house. "Morganne? Call your boss, check to see what kind of vehicle she drives."

As if reading his mind, she nodded quickly and pulled out her phone.

"I'm going to look into the other windows." Without waiting for her to respond, he went around to the back of the house, checking every window he passed.

When he came upon windows with heavy blinds covering them, he deduced they were Fisher's bedroom windows.

Unfortunately, the blinds were too tight for him to see anything. He hesitated, then continued checking all the other windows.

Every room he could see into was empty.

Except for the two bedroom windows, where he couldn't see in at all.

"She drives a Nissan Quest, which is a type of minivan." Morganne's light gray eyes were full of concern. "Do you think Blaine took it? Maybe after ditching the Impala?"

"Only one way to find out. The blinds over the bedroom windows are closed. I think we need to break into the house and make sure she's not being held against her will."

"Exigent circumstances," Morganne said with a nod. "Do it."

Using his boot heel, he kicked at the front door. The dead bolt must not have been engaged, because it opened after the first kick.

Pulling his weapon, he crossed the threshold. The awful smell hit hard, but he forced himself to go all the way inside.

He stared in horror when he found Kay Fisher's body in her bed, a rope tied around her neck.

She was dead.

FIVE

Blaine's former girlfriend had been strangled.

Morganne swallowed hard, her stomach lurching as she looked at poor Kay Fisher's dead body. Strangling his victims had been Blaine's MO. She lightly fingered the small scar on her neck, remembering the bite of the rope.

"We should have gotten here sooner." Her voice was barely a whisper.

"She's been dead for at least twelve hours, maybe longer." Colt took her arm. "The person who did this might be Blaine, but we can't rule out a copycat. We need to call your boss, get the crime scene tech in here."

So many crime scenes. She gladly backed

away from the bedroom and stumbled outside, gulping breaths of fresh air.

The Jackson PD wasn't used to having this much crime. Oh, sure they had the usual drinking and driving, drugs, fights, that kind of thing. But gunfire? Murder? No, this wasn't normal.

Five years ago, when Blaine had begun his killing spree, the Jackson PD had called in the FBI.

She could easily imagine her lieutenant being told by the chief of police to do that again, now. And honestly, she couldn't blame him.

"Are you okay?" Colt's gentle voice had her straightening her spine.

"Yes. It's not my first dead body." And she had a horribly bad feeling it wouldn't be her last. Not as long as Blaine was on the loose. "You don't really see this as a copycat, do you?"

"I prefer to keep all possibilities in mind," Colt said. "But that doesn't mean Winston isn't our top suspect."

"Why do you think she's been dead for at least twelve hours?"

"Because of the minivan." Colt cast his gaze over the area. "Let's assume Blaine came to Kay for help. She told him to get lost, so he forces his way inside, kills her and helps himself to her car keys. A few hours later, he comes after you."

"He shoots but misses and gets away in Kay's van," she finished his theory. She grabbed her phone to call her boss. "Lieutenant? Issue a Be on the Lookout for a Nissan Quest, registered to Kay Fisher." She rattled off the license plate she'd gotten a few minutes ago. A BOLO would alert every officer on duty, increasing the opportunity to find the vehicle. "We also need a squad and the medical examiner sent to Kay's address. We found her murdered and believe Blaine Winston is still in the area, driving her vehicle."

Her boss muttered something harsh. "Okay, will do. If this keeps up, the chief will call the Feds in to help."

"Yes, sir. Keep in mind, Colt Nelson is a US deputy marshal, and therefore a Fed. I'll see if he has additional resources for us."

"You do that." Her boss abruptly disconnected without saying anything more.

She understood his concern. Jackson, Wyoming, wasn't a large city like their state capital, Cheyenne. And they were already stretched to the max. A smart man knew when he was drowning and called for a lifeboat.

Her only concern was that the FBI tended to take over without being fully cooperative in return.

"I'm happy to call my boss and see if he can free up resources for us," Colt said. "Although I hate to sound like a broken record, but we don't have proof that Blaine is the one who killed Kay, or that he stole her car."

"Who else would do such a thing?" Morganne felt her temper slip.

Colt raised his hand in a gesture of surrender. "Look, I agree Winston is the main suspect. All I'm pointing out is that we don't have proof. We could use some DNA or other forensic evidence."

"Blaine strangled his victims, exactly the way Kay was murdered. And a killer's MO is often used as evidence," she pointed out.

"Yet we have reason to believe Silas had been injured in a way that caused bleeding in the shed, maybe with a knife or some other sharp object. And you were fired at, twice."

Yeah, she hated that she couldn't argue his point. "If the FBI is brought into the case, they'll run right over us."

"I know, and I don't want that any more than you do. Give me a few minutes to see what my boss thinks." He glanced to where a squad car was racing toward them, red lights and sirens blaring. "You handle the locals."

She watched as Colt walked away, speaking into his phone. As Officer Abrams slid out of the squad, she waved him over. "Victim is in the master bedroom, the one on the left."

"This related to the gunfire outside the Wagon Wheel?" Abrams eyed her with concern. "Seems like trouble is following you, Kimball."

"I'm convinced these events are related. The victim is Blaine Winston's old girlfriend, and her Nissan Quest is missing from her garage. According to the marshal, he believes the victim's time of death to be at least twelve hours ago or more." As she spoke, the coroner's truck rolled up behind the squad. "The ME will tell us for sure."

"I need to set up a perimeter. Boss wants everything done by the book." Abrams went to work, stretching crime scene tape from the mailbox at the foot of the driveway to a nearby tree.

She greeted Dr. Sapporo, the medical examiner, with a nod. "Victim is Kay Fisher, and she's inside. I'll show you."

The doctor followed her through Kay's modest house to the master bedroom. There, he donned gloves and performed a basic exam. "Cause of death appears to be strangulation, based on the petechial hemorrhaging in her eyes and the ligature marks around her neck. Of course, this opinion could change once I perform the autopsy and get her toxicology results."

"Any idea how long she's been dead?" Morganne asked, breathing through her mouth in an effort not to throw up.

"I'd say she died around midnight last night, give or take an hour. Again, that depends on the tox screen and anything else I find in the postmortem."

Last night, just as Colt surmised. "Okay, thank you." She retreated from the crime scene, joining Colt on the street. "You were right about the time of death," she said. "Doc thinks midnight, give or take."

Colt's expression looked grim. "Crane is going to try to get us help, but there's no guarantee. The lack of evidence…" He shrugged. "We need proof Winston was here."

Logically, she understood. Emotionally, she wanted to snap. She drew in a calming breath. "Okay, so how do we get that evidence? Short of arresting the guy, which is top priority in my book."

Colt glanced at his watch. "We need to talk to Neal Henderson, our eyewitness. Only we can't do that for another couple of hours. In the meantime, we should grab some lunch and use that time to review the receipts from the Wagon Wheel."

Food? Her stomach rolled. "Not sure I'm up to eating."

"Kimball?" Abrams waved her over as he put his phone away. "Lieutenant asked me to let you know they found a shell casing in the woods behind the Wagon Wheel. Looks to be a thirty aught six, same caliber as was found outside your place."

A flicker of hope brightened her eyes. "Lift any fingerprints?" If they had prints that belonged to Blaine, they'd have the proof Colt needed.

"Nope. None on the shell from your place, either." Abrams noted her crest-fallen features. "Hey, we'll find him. We're sending the casings out to verify they were fired from the same gun."

It was a step in the right direction, but it wasn't enough. "Great, thanks." She turned toward Colt. "I guess there's nothing more we can do here. We should probably hike back to your SUV."

"And then get lunch," he repeated, falling into step beside her. "It's going on one o'clock, and our breakfast was hours ago."

"You're obsessed with eating," she muttered as they took the quickest route back to his SUV. Since Kay had been dead for a while, it wasn't likely Blaine would be sitting and waiting for them, but she noticed Colt swept his gaze around to make sure.

She did the same. This wasn't the time to underestimate the guy who'd killed at least four people, maybe more, without blinking an eye.

They arrived at the SUV without an issue, but Colt held up his hand, warning her to stay back. She frowned, then lifted a brow when he removed a small device from beneath the SUV.

"What is that?" She stepped forward to peer at it.

"A small car alarm. Sends out a shriek if someone tries to tamper with the car when we're not here." He grinned. "It's a new device, still in beta testing, but personally, I think it's ready for prime time."

"Hmm." She could see how the device would be helpful. "Does it send out an electrical shock, zapping the person tampering with the car?"

Colt burst out laughing. "No, but that's a good idea. I'll pass your suggestion along to the design team."

She couldn't help but smile at his laughter and felt lighter for the first time since her lieutenant woke her up in the middle of the night.

Working alongside Colt provided a sense of camaraderie she hadn't experienced in a long time.

"Where's a good place to eat around here?" He glanced at her expectantly.

The man was all about food. "We could go back to the Wagon Wheel, but there's a small café that's better. I usually stop in about once a week. It has typical sandwiches, breakfast food and usually a special or two."

"Works for me. Rhonda's Café? I think I saw it on the way over."

"Yep, that's the one." She had to give Colt credit for having good observation skills. "Rhonda is a great cook."

Five minutes later, Colt pulled up in front of the café. After gathering up the receipts from the Wagon Wheel, he once again quickly placed the small alarm on the vehicle, then followed her inside.

There was an open booth, so she grabbed

it. Colt dropped down across from her, set the stack of receipts on the table and grabbed the menu. "What do you recommend?"

"I haven't had a bad meal yet." She was a little surprised her appetite was returning. "The butter burgers will give you a heart attack, but they're amazing."

"Sold." Colt set the menu aside. "What are you having?"

"The chicken salad sandwich is good." Their server came with two ice waters and took their order. Morganne leaned forward. "Did you really scope out this place on the way over to Kay's house?"

A hint of red darkened his cheeks, but he nodded. "Yeah, I did."

She smiled and shook her head in amazement. "That's a little obsessive."

He lifted his clear green eyes to hers, a serious expression settling over his features. "I grew up very poor. My mom barely scraped by, even working two jobs. I never knew if there would be any dinner when I came home and often went to bed hungry."

"Oh, Colt." She quickly reached across the table to take his hand. "I'm so sorry. I shouldn't have teased you like that. It was completely insensitive."

The corner of his mouth lifted in a smile. "Don't beat yourself up, Morganne. My buddies give me grief about my obsession with meals all the time. I never told them the real reason and, well—I don't know why I dumped that on you. Chalk it up to a lack of shut-eye."

"I am beating myself up, Colt. I was often teased in high school—being tall, thin, flat as a board and redheaded like a clown was enough for the kids to pick on me. I didn't like it then, and I shouldn't have resorted to the same tactics now."

"It's not the same thing." His brow furrowed. "I'm sorry you had to go through that, Morganne. I bet those same guys are kicking themselves now, because you've grown into a beautiful woman."

It was her turn to flush with embarrassment. She knew Colt was only trying to be nice, especially after she'd jammed her foot into her mouth in a big way.

But it was a sweet gesture, and it had been a long time since anyone had been nice to her. Her one and only serious relationship, with a guy named Raymond Natter, had ended badly after Blaine's attack. Ray had dumped her, as if she were soiled goods. Or maybe because he was worried she could toss him over her shoulder like a sack of bricks.

Somehow, she sensed Colt would never do something like that. He was strong and protective. Yet she knew better than to let her guard down. She wasn't opening herself up to be hurt like that again.

Besides, her partnership with Colt was temporary. As soon as they'd found and arrested Blaine, Colt would be assigned a new case.

Leaving her and the Wyoming dust far behind.

* * *

Colt sipped his water and methodically made his way through his stack of receipts as Morganne did the same. It was a useless effort, though—he didn't find anything of interest.

He shoved them aside, glancing at Morganne. Why had he bared his soul to her? Slade and Tanner didn't know anything about how he'd grown up hungry, and they were his closest friends.

Their teasing had always been easy to shrug off, maybe because he could give it right back to them. Tanner was habitually late, and Slade had trouble learning to let things go. They'd ribbed each other mercilessly, and it had never bugged him.

Hearing about how Morganne had been teased as a youth bothered him. A lot. It made him want to find those who'd ridiculed her and punch them in the nose.

Well, not really. He wasn't violent by nature. Still, he hated that she'd had to go through that.

And actually, her turning into a stunning, strong, smart and capable cop was the best way for her to put the past behind her. Although that did raise the question…

"Were you being honest when we first met last night? You know, about not having a man in your life?" As soon as he'd asked, he felt stupid. "Not that it's any of my business."

"Yes, I was being honest, even though you're right that it really isn't any of your business." She smiled wryly and set her receipt pile aside. "I didn't think it would be a smart move to lie to a federal marshal."

That made him chuckle. "Hey, if it makes you feel better, you know more about me than a lot of people. To be honest, my job sends me to a variety of states, so having a relationship isn't easy. But you're local, Morganne. Makes me think the guys around this town are all dumber than boxes of rocks."

"There's no need to go overboard with the flattery," she said. "Oh, and I didn't find anything in these receipts. Looks like you didn't, either."

"Nope." Before he could tell her he wasn't flattering her, their server returned to their booth with two plates of food. His stomach growled at the enticing scent of his medium-rare butter burger.

Bring on the heart attack, he thought, eyeing his plate. He grinned at their server. "Looks great, thanks."

"For sure," Morganne agreed.

He bowed his head, silently thanking God for the food and the company. When he lifted his head, he found Morganne eyeing him curiously.

"I like to pray before eating."

"Because every meal is a gift?" Her observation was right on the mark.

"Yes." He shifted uncomfortably in his seat. Like his past, he didn't often talk about his faith to others. "We should always be grateful for what we have."

"You're right, we should." Morganne picked up her chicken salad sandwich.

"My mother attended church regularly, but after she died, my dad and I pretty much stopped going."

"I'm sorry to hear that." He reached over to touch her hand. "Losing a parent is hard. My mom has been gone for the past five years."

"Did you know your dad?" Morganne asked.

"No. Mom said he took off when I was a baby. To my knowledge, she never bothered to track him down to divorce him or to get child support payments." He shrugged. There had been times when he'd railed at the man who'd abandoned them, especially when they'd run out of food. But his mother had always insisted that his father was the one who'd lost out by not knowing them, and they were better off without him.

God asked them to forgive those who trespassed against them. He'd done his best to do that. And he'd run across some really bad men, those who killed without an ounce of remorse.

It made him realize his mother was right—they'd been much better off without his father.

He tried not to wolf down his food—another bad habit from when he was growing up. He flushed when he caught Morganne watching him. "Do I have ketchup on my face or what?"

"No, sorry." Her cheeks went pink. "I—um, was thinking about what our next move should be."

He doubted it but went along with the change of subject. "You mean after we talk to Neal?"

"Or before that," she said with a sigh. "It feels like we're pinning all of our hopes on a bartender."

She made a good point. Even if Neal Henderson reiterated the man he saw was Blaine Winston, they needed to figure out what to do with that information. He wasn't convinced Crane would free up

Slade Brooks and Tanner Wilcox to help them out. Especially since there was a slim possibility that Winston had hightailed it out of Wyoming in Kay's Nissan Quest.

Although he doubted it. His gut told him Winston was here solely to kill Morganne. And he doubted the guy would leave until the task was done.

But why? That was the question. Because she was the one who'd gotten away? And had helped him get arrested? Was this really all about revenge?

Colt's thoughts swirled as he ate every bite of his burger and downed every french fry. He wasn't one to leave uneaten food on his plate, and he noticed Morganne finished hers, too.

"Can I interest you in dessert?" Their server came by to refill their water glasses. "We have a freshly baked peach pie topped with vanilla ice cream."

Just the thought of peach pie made his mouth water, but he managed to resist temptation. "Not for me, thanks. Morganne?"

"I'm sorry, but I couldn't possibly eat another bite."

"We'll take the check when you have a minute." He waited until she'd left them alone to lean forward. "You mentioned a couple of Blaine's old rodeo pals, Vince Lange and Owen Plumber. I know they were vetted when he first escaped, but a lot of time has passed. I say we try to reach out to them, see if they know where he is."

She nodded slowly. "That's a good idea."

"Okay, then as soon as we're paid up..." A loud screeching sound cut him off midsentence—his car alarm. He leaped up and raised his voice so he could be heard over the obnoxious noise. "Everyone get down!"

Patrons dropped to the floor. Pulling his weapon, Colt crouched down and made his way to the diner's large window overlooking the parking lot. Too bad he didn't have his binoculars.

The area around his SUV was clear, but that didn't necessarily mean anything.

Had the alarm gone off by accident? Someone bumping into his car?

Or had Winston found them?

SIX

Making sure to stay low, Morganne crept over to where Colt was looking through the window. “See him?”

“No.” He frowned, then sighed. “Could be nothing, but I’m going to check it out.”

“I’ll cover you.” She drew her weapon, partially aware of the café patrons crying out and huddling beneath the tables. “Nothing to worry about,” she called loudly. “We’re simply taking extra precautions.”

“Stay here.” Colt headed toward the doorway. Annoyed with his directive, she followed hot on his heels.

What part of working as partners didn’t he understand? Partners backed each other up, no matter what.

Colt disappeared through the doorway, darting toward his SUV. She took up a position in the doorway and swept her gaze over the area, trying to catch a glimpse of sunlight off a rifle scope.

She didn't see anything unusual. Seconds later, the shrieking alarm was silenced, which only made the crying and raised voices from inside the café sound louder.

"All clear," Colt called.

She rose and turned back to the café patrons. "Sorry for the false alarm. Try to have a good day."

The murmuring voices grew softer, and most of the crying stopped as people realized they were safe. She saw their server hovering in the corner and gestured her over. "How much was our meal?"

The trembling woman handed her the bill. Morganne quickly paid and headed outside to where Colt was still searching the area around the SUV.

"Any idea what set it off?"

"No." His gaze was wary. "We should get out of here, just in case."

"Seems like the car alarm isn't all it's cracked up to be." She opened the passenger door and climbed inside.

Colt slid in behind the wheel. "Well, it executed its main job, which is to let us know if anyone touches the SUV. Whether that was friend or foe remains to be seen."

She glanced at him curiously. "You really think Blaine set it off?"

"Probably not," he conceded. "But we need to remain alert. If the shooter is Winston, and he's still in the area, he'll make another attempt against you."

As much as she wasn't buying the copycat theory, she knew Colt was right to keep an open mind. She kept coming back to the fact that her cousin had been free for nine long months. He'd always been arrogant, but it was still a risk to return to the scene of his original crimes.

To target the same victim, in coming after her.

It still didn't make sense.

Although neither did the copycat killer theory. Colt had mentioned not knowing about Kay Fisher's personal life, so she used her phone to check the woman's social media pages.

"Looks like Kay was seeing a guy named Doug Levine." She stared for a moment at the photo of the pair. Maybe it was her imagination, but it seemed as if Kay's smile was forced. And Doug wasn't smiling at all. "I'll let my boss know they should check out this Doug Levine guy, make sure he has an alibi for the time frame of the murder."

"Good idea. Winston may have killed her somewhere else and brought her to the house. Hopefully, they'll find her Nissan soon."

"With Blaine behind the wheel," she added.

"That would be great," Colt said with a weary smile.

She sincerely hoped Blaine was still in

Jackson. If he'd left town, it could take days to find him. Weeks, or months if he'd somehow gotten a different vehicle.

The thought of Blaine eluding law enforcement yet again made her feel sick to her stomach. She couldn't, wouldn't let that happen.

"I'm going to stay at my place tonight." The statement popped out without her thinking it through.

"What?" Colt stared at her. "You can't. Winston will look for you there."

"If he's still in town, if he's the shooter and if he's Kay's killer, then yeah. That's the plan." She lifted her chin and narrowed her gaze. "The sooner we grab him, the safer everyone will be. Did you see those people inside the café? They were crying and hiding beneath their tables, fearing some sort of Wild West shoot-out. This town survives on tourism, and gunfire tends to put a damper on recreational activities."

"You're not using yourself as bait." Colt's hard, flat tone only fueled her anger.

"It's not your decision." She glanced at the slip of paper with Neal Henderson's address. "Turn right at the next road."

"Morganne, you need to think this through." Ignoring her directions, Colt pulled off to the side of the road and threw the gearshift into Park. "You can't just go home for the night without a plan. We need to have a slew of cops available to surround your place."

She lifted a hand. "Blaine will never show if he stumbles across a cop stationed every few yards. He needs to believe I'm home alone, or this won't work."

"Not happening." Colt's face was stone.

This wasn't the time or place to have this conversation. She understood and appreciated his concern for her welfare, but his lack of trust in her abilities was disheartening. She'd managed to get away from Blaine once, and that was when he'd caught her unexpectedly, alone and outside a restaurant.

Doubtful he'd escape again if she was lying in wait for him.

"Let's head over to Neal's place," she said, changing the subject. "Looks like he lives in an apartment. He should be up by now if he has to work at three thirty. After what happened with Kay, I'm feeling the need to check in on him, make sure he's okay."

Colt appeared to be wrestling with his temper, but his voice didn't show it. "Fine, we'll head over to talk to our witness. But this conversation isn't over."

Yeah, it was, but there was no point in arguing. She was free to spend the night wherever she wanted, and there was nothing he could do about it.

Except possibly back her up, if he'd go along with her idea.

If not, well, she'd handle it on her own.

She continued offering Colt directions until they were in front of the small two-story, four-family building. According to what Cully White had told them, Neal's apartment was on the first floor.

After entering the building, they found and knocked on his door. A minute later, the door opened, revealing a sleepy-eyed man in his midtwenties. He blinked as they offered their badges.

"Oh, you're here about that tip I called in on that 1-800 crime stoppers number." Neal jammed his fingers through the hair sticking out of his head at odd angles. "Uh, come in."

"Thanks," Morganne said, stepping through the doorway. Tidiness wasn't high on Neal's list of priorities, although she supposed working nights and closing the Wagon Wheel meant he didn't have a lot of extra time. "Sorry to bother you so early, Mr. Henderson."

"Call me Neal." The kid grimaced. "The only Mr. Henderson in the family is my old man."

"As Officer Kimball said, we really appreciate you taking the time to talk to us." Colt smiled. "We're obviously very interested in hearing more about why you believe you saw Blaine Winston last night."

"Yeah, okay." Neal sank down on the edge of his sofa. Morganne perched near him, while Colt stood. "I work the three-thirty-to-close shift," Neal began. "This guy came in, all by himself, and took a seat at the end of the bar. He didn't talk to anyone at first, just ordered his Jack and Coke and slammed it back."

"He seemed upset in some way?" Morganne asked.

"Well, maybe more tired and crabby," Neal said. "Not mad, but not in a good mood, that's for sure."

"What did he say to you?" Morganne pressed.

Neal shrugged. "Nothing, really, other than ordering his drinks. Gave off the leave-me-alone vibe."

She exchanged a glance with Colt. Back when they were younger, Blaine hadn't been a loner. He'd always chatted with people, even those he didn't know. There was no denying that being a fugitive from the law could have changed that personality trait. But Neal's description still didn't quite mesh with the Blaine she knew.

"What did he look like?" Colt asked.

"Short dark hair with a widow's peak, blue eyes and a black cowboy hat. He also had a small scar along his chin." Neal smiled. "That scar was what caught my attention, because I have a similar scar." The bartender pointed to the right side of his jaw. "Some idiot hit me with a beer bottle."

Again, the scar and widow's peak were consistent with Blaine Winston's facial features. Although Morganne knew that Blaine's scar had come from his rodeo days, not a beer bottle. "How tall was he?"

"Six feet two inches tall." Neal rose to his feet. "I'm six feet two inches as well, and we were staring eye to eye before he took a seat at the bar."

Morganne frowned. “Are you sure about that? Six feet two inches?”

“Positive.” Neal frowned. “Why, is that wrong?”

She forced a smile. “Nothing is right or wrong, Neal. We’re just trying to validate all the details.”

“I’m telling you, this guy was Blaine Winston,” Neal insisted.

“Why are you so convinced?” Colt asked.

“Because someone called out the name Wilson, and the guy flinched and glanced over his shoulder. He looked nervous and then tossed money on the bar and left.” Neal glanced between them. “I remembered reading about Blaine Winston’s killing spree five years ago and went online to check out the story, which included a picture of his mug shot. He looks different now in some ways, face narrower and leaner, different hair color, but overall I’m positive it’s the same guy. That’s why I called the toll-free number to make the report.”

"Thanks, Neal, you've been very helpful." Morganne slowly rose to her feet.

"Should I—uh, let you know if he shows up again?" Neal asked.

"Absolutely. Here's my contact information." Colt handed Neal his business card. "Please don't hesitate to call 911 first, though. This man is armed and dangerous."

"Okay, I'll do that." Neal tucked the card into his jeans. "I hope you find him."

"We will." Morganne infused confidence in her tone. "Thanks again."

When they were back outside, Colt eyed her thoughtfully. "Okay, what's wrong?"

"Blaine's hair was blond when I knew him, but he easily could have dyed his hair. My biggest concern is that there's no way he's six feet two inches tall." She went over to stand beside Colt. "That's about your height, too, isn't it?"

"Yeah." He frowned. "Why? What are you getting at?"

"I'm five feet nine inches tall." She

tipped her head slightly to look him in the eye. “Blaine is only five-ten. I know this for certain from the night he grabbed me from behind. I was able to fight him off, first by slamming my head into his face, busting his nose, and then because of my martial arts skills and training.”

Colt nodded slowly. “If he was taller, your head would have hit his chin, not his nose.”

“Exactly. Afterward, I learned his first three victims were petite and therefore more easily overpowered.” She sighed and tried to think logically. “Neal sounded like a good witness. He had the description of Blaine’s scar down pat, and Blaine does have a widow’s peak in his hairline. But the height isn’t right. And changing that by a good four inches isn’t easy.”

Colt scowled. “Not easy, but not impossible. And maybe Neal was off by an inch or two.”

“Maybe.” A wave of exhaustion hit hard as she pulled the passenger door open.

They were no closer to catching Blaine now than they had been earlier that morning. Which meant she needed to follow through on her plan to use herself as bait.

She would do whatever it took to put an end to this manhunt.

Colt tried to imagine Winston wearing hiking boots with lifts in them. It wasn't unreasonable to assume the guy had tried to change his appearance.

Yet why not use a little makeup to minimize the scar? It was difficult to make sense of Neal's observations, yet Morganne was right about the guy being a decent witness.

"We should have Neal work with a sketch artist," he said, breaking the silence.

"Good idea. I'll call my lieutenant and see if he can get that arranged."

Colt drove slowly through Jackson, listening as Morganne made the call. He was glad she placed the call on speaker so he could hear both sides of the conversation.

"The bartender is a good witness," Morganne said. "It would be a good idea to arrange for him to work with Barb, our sketch artist."

There was a heavy sigh. "Yeah, okay, I'll add that to the list."

"We also found out Kay Fisher has a boyfriend, a guy by the name of Doug Levine. I know you've been swamped, but any idea if he has an alibi for the time of Kay's murder?"

Colt could hear the lieutenant typing on a keyboard. "Yeah, I asked Officer Yevich to swing by his place of employment to talk to him. Levine works at one of those dude ranches outside town."

"That's great. It would be good to check Levine off the list of suspects." Morganne glanced at Colt. "No sign of Kay's Nissan Quest? Or Silas Winston's Chevy Impala?"

"No, but I'll be honest, my resources are stretched pretty thin. We don't have many officers left doing basic patrol."

"I know." A flash of guilt darkened Morganne's gray eyes. "But you've looped in the state patrol, right?"

"Of course." The lieutenant's voice was testy. "And if we don't find this guy soon, I've been told to call in the FBI first thing Monday morning."

Colt winced but didn't protest. Morganne looked similarly dismayed. "I understand. We'll keep looking for him. If he's here in Jackson, we'll find him."

"Do it, and soon."

"Yes, sir. If you need something, let me know."

"Hang on, Kimball. Just got a text message from Yevich. He's at the Sundown Ranch and has learned Kay's boyfriend, Doug Levine, didn't show up for work today."

"Really?" Morganne's eyebrows lifted in surprise. "Is Yevich heading to Levine's home?"

"Yep. Look, I gotta go, the chief is calling." The lieutenant abruptly cut off the call.

"Didn't show up for work, huh?" Colt glanced at her. "That sounds a bit suspicious."

"It does, yes. But he could just be sick or something, right?" She didn't sound convinced.

"True." Colt prided himself on keeping an open mind, but deep down, he was fairly certain Winston was the guy who'd killed Kay Fisher. He swallowed a frustrated sigh. "I guess we'll learn more once your fellow cop heads to his place. For all we know this is nothing more than Levine sleeping off a late night of partying. It would explain how Winston found Kay home alone."

Morganne didn't say anything, her gaze focused on some point in the distance. Finally she turned toward him. "Are we wrong about all this being related to Blaine?"

"I don't think so. At least, that's what my gut is telling me. But getting to the truth is the point of doing an investigation, right?"

"Right." She shook her head. "There isn't anyone else I can think of who'd want to shoot me through my bedroom window."

"And that was the starting point of this." Well, technically, Kay Fisher's murder may have come first. And when exactly had Silas been injured? Was he still alive, being held hostage by Blaine? Or had he already been killed, his usefulness over? They needed to follow up with the Rock Springs police department to request additional information from that crime scene.

In his mind, all roads led straight to Blaine Winston. Neal had either gotten the guy's height wrong, or the killer had added lifts to his shoes, but the longer Colt stayed in Jackson, the more he believed Winston was here, doing his best to hide in plain sight.

"Where to?" He glanced at Morganne questioningly. "Any ideas?"

"Maybe we drive around a bit, see if we can spot the Nissan. I have the license plate number on my phone." She grimaced. "After talking to my boss, I'm feeling guilty not being out on patrol. No small surprise that no one has spotted it yet."

"No reason to feel guilty. We're actively working the case," he reminded her. "We found Kay's body and interviewed the eyewitness. Trust me, we're doing our part to help find Winston."

"There is that," she agreed. "We also need to check in with Blaine's old buddies, Vince Lange and Owen Plumber. But pull over, would you? I need a few minutes to find their addresses."

"Not a problem—" His comment was cut short by the crack of gunfire, followed by the shattering of their rear window.

"Go!" Morganne shouted, ducking down in her seat.

He hit the gas hard. The SUV responded by leaping forward, the rear wheels spinning and catching on the asphalt.

The second shot hit one of the rear tires, sending the SUV careening out of control. As they slid sideways and landed in a ditch, Colt prayed God would keep them safe.

And that Blaine wouldn't reach them before they could get away.

SEVEN

Even though she was wearing her seat belt, Morganne's head sharply struck the side of the window as the SUV rolled down into the ditch. For a moment she didn't move, but then the reality of their tenuous situation spurred her into action.

"Colt? Are you okay?" She unfastened her seat belt and grabbed his arm. He looked as grim as she felt. "We have to get out of here."

"I'm okay." There was blood on his temple, probably from flying glass. He turned in his seat to face her. "My door is blocked by the ditch. We'll need to go out on your side."

She pushed her door open, hearing the grinding of metal against metal. After scrambling through the opening, she crouched next to the vehicle and covered Colt as he emerged. She marveled at how he'd taken a moment to grab the binoculars from the glove box.

"The shots came from behind us," she whispered. "We need to head west toward the mountains. I think that must be where he's hiding."

"I agree. But there isn't a lot of cover until we reach them," Colt cautioned. "Give me a minute to try to find him as we wait for backup."

"You can try to find him, but the department is stretched to the max. No way can we wait long enough for my lieutenant to free up officers from two crime scenes. We need to move, now, before Blaine gets away."

Colt didn't look happy, but he reluctantly nodded. He took precious minutes to peer through the binoculars before lowering them. "No sign of him yet. Follow me."

She watched as Colt darted from the vehicle to the closest tree, then from there to the corner of a garage. She followed his path, mentally braced for more gunfire while keeping a close eye out for any movement from the strip of mountainside.

They had to get to Blaine. They just had to!

Colt's zigzag pattern worked well, especially since he cut through several streets to approach the mountains from a different angle from where they'd left the damaged SUV. She was impressed with his skill and tenacity.

Her head throbbed as they moved through town, but she ignored it, remaining focused on finding Blaine. She was hoping he wouldn't expect them to come this way—maybe they'd catch him unaware.

Granted, he had the scope of his rifle with which to search for them. Colt paused periodically to use the binocs but gave no indication he'd located their target.

Twenty minutes later, they were huddled

in the brush at the base of the mountains. "No sign of him?" she whispered.

"No." He handed her the binocs. "See if you can spot something I may have missed."

She doubted he'd missed anything, but she took a moment to peer at the most likely high spots Blaine may have used as a perch to shoot from. There was an outcropping of rock about fifty yards from their current spot. She lowered the binocs. "I say we head over to that rock. It's the most likely place he'd have used."

"I noticed that, too," Colt agreed. "I doubt he's still up there."

"We won't know for sure until we check it out." She glanced at the nearby trees, most of which weren't strong enough to hold a man's weight. "Ready?"

Colt nodded and picked a path through the woods, heading up the slope to the outcropping of rock. They continued using various trees and brush for cover, pausing every so often to search through the binoculars.

Other than their movements, the area around them was unusually silent.

Colt hunkered down about ten yards from the rock outcropping and lifted the binocs to his eyes. For several long moments she didn't hear anything but the sound of their breathing from the exertion of climbing the hill.

"I don't see anything," Colt whispered, handing the glasses to her. "Check it out."

She did, her heart sinking as she moved the glasses over the area. If Blaine had used the spot as a shooting perch, he wasn't there now.

"He's gone," she whispered, battling a wave of frustration.

"Let's see if he left anything behind." Colt pocketed the binocs and headed toward the rock, still moving cautiously in case this was some sort of trap. She watched closely, expecting Blaine to jump out of the brush like some sort of monster.

But when they reached the rock, no one was there.

Morganne couldn't believe he'd gotten away yet again. When had Blaine turned into a master escape artist?

A few feet from the rock, she found another hiking-boot print. "Colt? This tread looks to be the same as what we found outside my place."

He joined her, looking down at the partial print as she used her phone to capture the image. "It is," he agreed. "While it could be a common brand of hiking boot, I'm not buying the coincidence. Same guy was here, no doubt about that. And this was his third attempt to shoot you in less than twenty-four hours."

She was grimly aware of that fact. On one hand, shooting with a rifle from a distance wasn't Blaine's MO. Then again, she figured he knew she'd successfully escaped his clutches before. This was probably his way of getting rid of her once and for all.

From a safe and, in her opinion, cowardly distance.

"Hey, look at this."

She glanced over to where Colt was kneeling beside the rock. Using a stick, he pried something from a crevasse.

"What is it?"

"Another shell casing." When he had freed the brass, he carefully used the stick to lift it up. "Our guy has been sloppy, leaving brass at every single place he's used as a hiding spot."

She had to admit, it was encouraging. A hiking-boot print was nothing, but that along with the casing made her think they'd found Blaine's lookout. "It's also from a thirty aught six, just like the others."

"Yep." He rummaged in his pocket and found a plastic baggie. Dropping the brass inside, he grinned with satisfaction. "Once all three casings are compared and proven to be fired from the same weapon, we'll have more evidence to use against him."

He was right, but she also knew it wasn't enough. Not to prove the shooter was Blaine and not some other random criminal out to seek revenge against her. She sighed and tried to ignore the wave of exhaustion that typically followed the adrenaline crash. "Guess we should start hiking out of here."

Colt nodded and led the way down the side of the mountain. Much easier going down, except for the slippery spots. She lost her footing but managed to stay on her feet.

"We'll need someone to pick us up." Colt glanced at her over his shoulder. "A cop? Or a friend?"

Most of her friends were cops, so she nodded. "I'll call Nate."

"Nate who?" Colt asked sharply.

She frowned. "Nate Jamison. You met him at my place, remember? He works the graveyard shift, but he lives close by. I'm sure he'll help us."

"Oh, yeah. Jamison." Colt looked as if

he wanted to say something more, but he didn't.

Pulling out her phone, she stared at the screen. It was cracked from the wreck, but the phone still worked, at least in theory. Unfortunately, the corner of the screen indicated she had no service.

"Check your phone for service," she suggested. "I've got nothing yet."

Colt did and grimaced. "Nope."

Great. They continued making their way down the mountain until they were at street level. Now her phone showed several bars, so she quickly called Jamison's number.

"What?" he answered with a growl.

"Hey, sorry to wake you, but we need a lift. Gunman shot out the window of the marshal's SUV and it's crashed in a ditch. We're on Oakdale, which isn't far from you. We'll hike to your place."

"Yeah, okay." Nate didn't sound very excited.

"Listen, I'm sorry to wake you up so

early, but things have been escalating all day. I can fill you in when we get there."

"I have a few missed calls from the lieutenant," he admitted. "I'm sure he wants me to come in early."

"He needs all the help he can get, that's for sure. Thanks, Nate. We'll be there in about fifteen minutes."

"I thought you weren't seeing anyone?" Colt asked as she led the way to Jamison's house.

"I'm not." She frowned. If she didn't know better, she'd think he might be jealous. "We're just friends. We went through the police academy together."

"I see."

Did he really? She shook her head at his foolishness. "Nate is dating a woman named Stacy. I don't know how serious it is, but he seems happy with her."

"Oh." Colt looked embarrassed. "Sorry, I shouldn't have jumped to conclusions."

"Goofball," she muttered. Neither one of them spoke over the next ten minutes.

Soon she turned up the street leading toward Jamison's house. When they reached the small ranch, she rapped at the door.

Jamison greeted them dressed in his uniform, his hair damp from the shower. "Give me a minute. I need to put on my shoes and open the garage door."

Soon Nate drove his Chevy Blazer out of the garage. She and Colt climbed in. "Where to?" Nate asked.

"My place," Morganne said.

"No, the Mountain View Motel," Colt countered.

She turned to glare at him. "We need a car, right? Mine is sitting in my garage. Besides, isn't it time for us to play offense? As you said earlier, he's tried to shoot me three times in the past twenty-four hours. Enough is enough."

"Whoa, what's this? You said you'd fill me in," Nate interrupted.

Morganne briefly outlined what had happened since they'd last seen Nate. Colt also gave the cop the shell casing they'd found at the rock, requesting it be processed with the others.

"I can do that," Nate agreed.

"We need to do something to draw Blaine out of hiding," Morganne said.

"A woman has been murdered." Colt scowled. "I don't want you to be next."

"He has a point, Morganne," Nate chimed in.

"We need a vehicle and a place to stay. End of discussion." Morganne sat back in her seat, wishing Colt had even a minuscule amount of faith in her abilities to hold her own.

"Fine. Have it your way. We'll go to your place to get your vehicle." Colt's tone was testy. "We'll discuss our next move then."

She belatedly remembered their plan to find Vince and Owen. "Yeah, okay." She still planned to spend the night at her house, but in the meantime, they still had work to do.

So far, all they had was a dead former

girlfriend, three shell casings and several boot prints.

She'd find a way to convince Colt to spend the night at her place to draw Blaine out.

In her humble opinion, they needed to do something drastic to put an end to this once and for all.

Before he killed again.

He was feeling overprotective of Morganne, but being shot at multiple times tended to do that to a guy. Cop or not, Colt didn't like knowing she was at the center of Blaine's target.

Was this how his buddies Slade and Tanner had felt while protecting the women they cared about from danger? If so, he hadn't been sympathetic enough to their plight.

And man, he really wished his buddies were here with him now. They'd both taken less risky roles within the marshal service, but he knew they'd come if asked.

The drive to Morganne's place didn't take long. He used the time to contact James Crane and let his boss know about the gunfire and that he needed a replacement vehicle, sooner than later.

His boss agreed to send Tanner and Slade to help him but warned they wouldn't be there until tomorrow afternoon at the earliest.

It was better than nothing.

"Are you really staying here tonight?" Jamison asked as he pulled up to Morganne's house. The crime scene tape was still stretched across her doorway, but there were no officers present anywhere nearby.

"Yes." Morganne pushed her door open. "Thanks for the ride."

"We appreciate it," Colt added, following suit.

"I'll swing by as often as possible while I'm on patrol," Jamison said. "And you can always call me directly if you need something."

"Thanks." Morganne smiled before closing the door.

The familiarity between Jamison and Morganne shouldn't have bothered him. He'd already made a fool of himself by acting jealous, which was ridiculous. He wasn't interested in a relationship with Morganne—he'd given his heart to Abby.

Yet spending time with Morganne had made it difficult for him to remember Abby's features, much less hold on to the feeling of love they'd shared.

He fingered the injury on his temple and told himself that there was too much going on at the moment to worry about his unusual emotional response to Morganne. She was already heading into the garage, so he lengthened his stride to catch up.

"Are you sure you're up to visiting Vince and Owen?" He watched her carefully. "After the car crash and strenuous hike, a little rest is reasonable."

"We need to check on them." She hesitated in the garage, then crossed over to the connecting door. "Let me grab my keys."

"Wait, I'm coming with you." He didn't really think Winston was hiding inside, but he wasn't going to take the risk.

She opened the door, glanced around and went into the house. He followed, splitting off once they'd crossed the threshold.

Clearing the house didn't take long, and he was deeply relieved there was no sign anyone had been there recently.

Morganne rummaged through a drawer, pulled out a set of keys and headed back to the garage. Suppressing a sigh at her sheer stubbornness, he went along.

"The apartment building they both live in isn't far. They're not roommates, but it could be they're still friends, since they live in the same place." Morganne backed out of the garage. "Hopefully we can talk to both of these guys and eliminate them as suspects. And maybe even learn something more about Blaine's other friends."

"That would be nice." Colt sent up a

quick prayer that neither of these men were dead in their beds, the way Kay Fisher had been.

Less than ten minutes later, Morganne pulled up in front of a four-story apartment building. The building was old and looked worn, but based on the cars parked in the lot, it was relatively full of tenants.

"Let's try Owen first." Morganne led the way inside and peered at the mailbox labels until she found Owen Plumber's apartment number. Leaning on the buzzer didn't elicit a response, so they took the stairs to the second floor.

The guy didn't answer their knock, either. "We may need to break in, make sure he's okay," Colt said.

A woman poked her head out of the apartment next door. "You looking for Owen? He left a few days ago."

"You saw him?" Morganne asked, showing her badge.

"Yeah, why?" Now the woman looked suspicious.

"Oh, he's not in trouble. We're here doing a wellness check," Morganne assured her. "You don't happen to know Vince Lange, do you? He's upstairs on the third floor."

"Nope." The woman went back inside her apartment and shut the door.

"Well, let's try Vince's place," Morganne said. "At least it doesn't sound like Owen is in danger."

"Doesn't mean he's not a suspect," he pointed out.

"True." They took the stairs to the next level, only to get a similar lack of response. Since no one poked their head out, Morganne knocked on the apartments nearby until she found someone who claimed to have seen Vince less than an hour ago.

"Not enough for exigent circumstances," Morganne muttered.

"We'll try again tomorrow." He rubbed the back of his neck. "I'm getting hungry. Maybe we can pick up something to eat on the way home."

Her features softened. “Sure, that sounds good.”

They stopped at an Italian restaurant and ordered lasagna to go. Once they were back at her place, he walked the perimeter after Morganne turned off the breaker switch for the backyard lights.

When he joined her inside, he was keenly aware of a sense of intimacy as they sat next to each other at the table. The lasagna smelled incredible as he bowed his head to pray.

He glanced up in surprise when Morganne reached over to touch his arm. “Would you pray out loud?”

“Ah, sure.” He didn’t pray out loud normally, but he went ahead to take her hand. “Lord, we thank You for this food we are about to eat. We ask that You continue to keep us safe and provide us the wisdom and strength we need to arrest this man. Amen.”

“Amen.”

They ate in silence for several moments. Morganne yawned widely, looking at him sheepishly. "I think the long day is catching up to me."

"Me, too." He smiled with understanding. "We'll call it an early night and get back to work first thing tomorrow."

"Yeah." Her brow furrowed. "Although I'm really hoping Blaine shows up here tonight."

I'm not, he thought wearily.

He walked the perimeter of her house for a second time as she washed the dishes. No sign of anyone lurking nearby, but it was early yet, barely nine o'clock.

When he went back inside, he found a pillow and a blanket on the edge of the sofa. Morganne's bedroom door was closed, so he sank onto the sofa, stretched out and stared up at the ceiling. He hadn't intended to fall asleep, but he must have, because a muffled cry woke him up.

Morganne! He bolted off the sofa, grabbed his gun and quickly ran to her door, praying Winston hadn't gotten to her while he was asleep.

EIGHT

"Are you okay?" Morganne abruptly sat up when Colt burst into her room. He raked his gaze over her, a wild look in his eye. "I heard you cry out."

"I—uh, sorry." She put a hand to her neck where she wore a scar from the rope Blaine had tried to strangle her with. "I'm fine. Just had a bad dream."

Colt lowered his weapon and crossed over to her. "I was worried Winston had gotten to you."

"No." She tried to shake off the aftermath of the nightmare. "I escaped." Which was not what had transpired in her dream.

Colt tucked the gun in his waistband and sat beside her. "Yes, you did. Because you're smart and strong."

She swallowed hard, her throat tight, as if the rope was still there. It had been months since she'd had the once-reoccurring nightmare of being strangled. She'd hoped one day it would go away completely, but it seemed the recent events, especially finding Kay's dead body, had brought the memories back in full force.

She drew in a deep breath in an attempt to calm her racing heart. Colt wrapped his arm around her shoulders, and she leaned gratefully against him. It was important to be viewed as a strong and capable cop, but at the moment she was simply a woman who'd survived a terrible attack.

"I'm sorry I woke you," she murmured.

"I'm glad I could be here for you." Colt tightened his arm around her. "Although I lost ten years off my life thinking Winston had gotten to you."

She knew Colt was still upset about how she'd insisted on returning to her place. Yet under the circumstances, she'd make the same decision again. She wanted, needed to arrest Blaine before he killed anyone else.

Colt pressed a gentle kiss on her temple, and she lifted her head to peer up at him through the darkness. His mouth was dangerously close, and without thinking it through, she kissed him.

His response was instantaneous, his mouth molding to hers as he deepened their kiss. All remnants of her nightmare faded away under the impact of their embrace.

If she were honest, she'd admit that she'd wanted to kiss him from the first moment she'd seen him, almost a year ago. Never had she imagined their paths would cross again.

Especially not like this.

He broke off their kiss but held her close. "I'm sorry if I took advantage of the situation," he finally whispered.

For some reason, his apology irked her. She pulled away and stared at him through the darkness. "It was just a kiss, Colt, nothing to apologize for." Especially as she'd initiated their embrace, not the other way around.

It was also completely uncharacteristic of her to do such a thing, especially after Ray had broken off their relationship after Blaine's attack. She'd silently promised never to risk her heart again and had focused her attention on her career.

Mentally annoyed with herself for succumbing to a moment of weakness, she eased away, putting more distance between them. "Sorry I woke you, but I'm fine now. Thanks."

"I—just didn't want you to get the wrong idea," Colt said. "I lost the love of my life years ago, and, well—I'm not ready to go down that path again."

The love of his life? "I'm sorry, I didn't realize."

"Abby helped me out back when I was in high school. We attended college together and planned to get married, but she was murdered in a carjacking."

She remembered him talking about the girl who'd supported him when he didn't have enough food to eat. "I understand, Colt. It's fine."

He looked a little uncertain as he rose and moved toward the door. "I'm here if you need anything. Good night, Morganne."

"Good night." When he closed the door behind him, she sighed and buried her face in her hands. The only good thing about what had just transpired was that it was now Colt's kiss and not the lingering nightmare that was front and center in her mind.

Not that reliving that toe-curling kiss would help her fall back to sleep. Especially after he'd informed her that he wasn't interested in her in that way. She should be used to men rejecting her by now. Shaking off the remorse, she rose and walked toward the bedroom window that wasn't boarded up.

Outside, her backyard looked peaceful

and serene, as if the gunfire of the previous night had never happened. Standing off to the side of the window, she surveyed the area for several long moments.

Where was Blaine? Had he finally left Wyoming in Kay's Nissan? Or was he still lurking nearby?

As she was about to turn away, a slight movement caught her eye. She froze and stared at the wooded area along the back of her property.

There!

A glimpse of a pale face was enough to have her sliding away from the window. She slid her feet into her running shoes and reached for her weapon.

"Colt," she whispered, emerging from the bedroom.

"I'm here." He eased up beside her. "What's going on?"

"I saw someone moving through the woods." She met his gaze. "We need to split up and investigate."

She braced for an argument, but he nodded in agreement. They moved silently through the house to the back door. She was glad she'd shut down the breaker switch so they could move through the darkness.

Although their position would be vulnerable as they crossed the open area of her backyard before reaching the woods. It seemed like a week had passed rather than twenty-four hours since they'd done this same thing.

Keeping low, she darted from the shadows and ran toward the group of trees. She noticed Colt mimicking her movement, heading toward the woods from the opposite side of the house.

She fully expected more gunfire, but the night remained eerily silent. Once she reached the cover of the trees, she took a moment to get her bearings before moving slowly through the brush.

The silence was unnerving. If she hadn't seen the movement and hint of a face with her own eyes, she'd believe this was nothing more than her wild imagination going haywire.

Or maybe that's what Blaine wanted her to think.

A shiver rippled down her spine as she continued moving through the woods. The low groan of a tree branch spurred her forward at the exact moment a man dropped to the ground beside her.

She reacted instinctively, lashing out with her foot and catching the guy in the abdomen. But her sneakered foot didn't pack enough of a punch, and he quickly recovered and charged forward, hitting her hard and sending her flying backward.

Her head hit the ground, sending jarring pain through her body, but she continued to fight, instinctively bringing her knee up and lashing out with her hand in a nose strike. His head snapped back and he grunted in pain, and then suddenly, he jumped up and took off running.

"Morganne?" Colt's shout sounded panicked. His footsteps pounded against the ground. "Are you okay?"

"Here," she wheezed, her chest tight from the hard landing. She pushed herself up to her feet, doing her best to ignore the pain. "Hurry! He's getting away!" She gestured in the direction he'd gone, estimating he'd continued through the woods to cut through the houses lining the other side of her property.

Colt took one more moment to scan her from head to toe before nodding and breaking into a run. She let him take the lead, covering his back while hoping and praying they'd catch up with Blaine.

But when they reached the houses that were located on the opposite side of the woods, there was no indication Blaine had come this way. Cutting between two houses, they reached the quiet and deserted road.

"Did you hear a car?" she asked between breaths.

"No, did you?" Colt swept his gaze back

and forth, making sure they hadn't missed something.

"No." She frowned. "How could we have lost him?"

"Let's go back to your place." Colt turned and retraced their steps.

She followed Colt, noting he was moving slower this time. She listened intently but didn't hear anything out of the ordinary.

Working together, they cleared the area surrounding her home and then went inside and cleared the interior.

"I don't get it." She scowled and put a hand to the bump forming on the back of her head. "How did he get away?"

"We should call this in and have cops search the entire neighborhood." Colt sighed, rubbing the back of his neck. "Even though I'm sure he's long gone by now."

"Yeah, probably." She reached for her phone and made the call to the dispatcher.

"Officer Jamison is two minutes away," the dispatcher informed her.

She went back outside to meet with her fellow officer. When he arrived, Nate listened intently as she described what happened.

"Did he say anything?" Colt asked.

"No." And she'd been surprised by that. She felt certain Blaine would have gloated over getting to her. "I hit him in the face, tried to break his nose, so we need to add that to his description going out over the news."

"Happy to do that," Jamison agreed. "Are you able to confirm the identity of your attacker? Did you get a good look at his face?"

"No." She thought back, bringing the images of the unexpected attack to her mind's eye. But it was dark and things had happened so fast. She was annoyed with herself for being caught off guard by Blaine dropping down from a tree, a move she should have anticipated. After all, they'd known he was up in a tree outside the Wagon Wheel and had shot at them from the rock. She needed to stop underestimating her cousin.

"Morganne?" Colt asked.

"No, I'm sorry, but between having the breath knocked out of me and hitting my head, I can't say for sure the attacker was Blaine."

"Did it seem like he was a stranger?" Colt pressed.

Once again, she thought back. "I wish I could be more definitive, but I can't." She blew out a breath. "You've been pressing for confirmation that Blaine is the one behind these incidents, but as it stands right now, I can't give that to you."

Colt looked frustrated, and she could relate.

Twenty-four hours had gone by, and they seemed to be exactly where they'd started.

With no way of proving Blaine was the one who'd come after her.

* * *

Colt noticed how Morganne was holding the back of her head and realized she must be hurt. “We should get you to a hospital.”

“No need, I’m fine.” She instantly dropped her hand. “It’s just a small bump.”

He frowned. “You might have a concussion.”

“I’m fine.” The stubborn edge to her tone made him swallow a sigh.

While Jamison searched the area where the assault had taken place, Colt went inside and found a bag of frozen veggies. He took it outside and pressed it into Morganne’s hand. “Use this as an ice pack.”

She rolled her eyes but lifted the bag to the back of her head.

Satisfied for now, Colt played his flashlight over the ground. “Here’s another hiking-boot print,” he said, kneeling beside it. “It appears to be the same tread we found yesterday.”

Jamison came over and nodded. “I agree.”

After photographing the evidence, they

continued searching but didn't find anything else.

Colt knew in his gut that Winston was the guy responsible for this most recent assault on Morganne. He couldn't bear to imagine what might have happened if he hadn't gotten there in time.

After an hour of searching, Jamison was called away. Colt escorted Morganne inside, gently nudged her into a kitchen chair and placed the bag of partially thawed veggies back in the freezer.

He sat across from her and scrubbed his hands over his face. "I guess your plan worked."

"Not really, since he got away." She sounded completely dejected. "I shouldn't have been caught off guard by him dropping down from a tree."

"Don't blame yourself, Morganne. This guy is awfully determined to exact his revenge. I'm just glad you aren't hurt worse than a bump on your head." The near miss made him feel sick to his stomach.

"Maybe his having an injured nose and a black eye will make it easier to find him," Morganne said glumly. "I mean, there can't be that many men walking around Jackson with fresh facial injuries."

"I agree, that should increase our ability to find him." He injected confidence in his tone. "We'll head out in a few hours, see if we can meet up with his former buddies. Maybe they'll give us something to go on."

"Yeah, maybe." She sighed. "I'm sorry, Colt. I guess this was a bad idea."

"Only because you were hurt, Morganne." He leaned forward. "I want to get Winston as much as you. But you need to be safe. What happened in the woods was a close call."

Too close.

"I know, and believe me, that wasn't part of the plan." She offered a lopsided smile. "Thanks for being so supportive."

"Of course. You know I care about you." Based on the spontaneous combustion of their kiss, he was glossing over his feelings in a big way. He'd told her about Abby as a way to hold her at bay, but it wasn't working. How he'd gotten so emotionally involved with her was a mystery.

One he didn't appreciate.

"It's barely four in the morning, so we should try to get some more sleep." Morganne stood and moved toward the hallway. "I doubt Blaine will return."

"I'm sure you're right about that. Good night." He had no intention of sleeping but wanted her to get some rest. That bump on her head was likely hurting more than she was letting on.

He prowled silently from one window to the next, making sure Winston didn't double back to finish what he'd started.

Three hours later, Morganne emerged from her room, freshly showered and breathtakingly beautiful.

"You look amazing. How's your headache?" Her hair was pulled back, but not as tightly as normal.

"Better, thanks." She crossed over to peer into her fridge. "I'm sorry, I don't have much food in here."

He hesitated, then said, "I noticed you have eggs and bread. I can whip up some French toast if you'd like."

She didn't take offense at his poking through her fridge. "Works for me. I even have maple syrup. But I'll make it if you'd like to shower."

"That would be great, thanks." He appreciated the offer.

Once they'd finished breakfast, he glanced at her. "Are you sure it's a good idea to use your Jeep? Does Winston know what you drive?"

"I have no idea if Blaine has gotten close enough to the house to know my car, but it's not as if we have a lot of options."

He glanced at his watch. "My buddies Slade and Tanner should be arriving sometime this afternoon. We can just sit tight and wait for them to pick us up."

She frowned. "Sit around and wait? No.

We still need to check in on Owen and Vince. Let's go."

He groaned inwardly but didn't argue. While he understood her need to keep working the case, it seemed likely Winston would be keeping an eye out for her Jeep.

The same way Winston had found and shot at his SUV.

"Ready?" Morganne had strapped on her shoulder harness and was striding toward the door leading to her garage.

Colt swallowed his protest and accompanied her out to the Jeep. Minutes later, they were heading back toward the apartment building where both Owen Plumber and Vince Lange lived.

He found it interesting that the two guys lived in the same building and theorized that Winston may have known right where to find his former rodeo buddies all these years later.

As before, knocking at each apartment

door yielded nothing in response. Colt stood back and surveyed the building.

"What are you thinking?" Morganne asked.

"That we need a search warrant." He pulled out his phone.

"On what grounds?" Morganne asked.

"That's a good question." He waited for his boss, James Crane, to pick up. "We have a known location for two of Winston's former associates. No answer at their respective apartments last night or this morning. It could be that one of these guys is aiding and abetting a fugitive from the law."

Crane sighed heavily into his ear. "That's a stretch, don't you think?"

"Listen, we already found Winston's former girlfriend dead. For all we know, one of these guys is dead, too."

"No one has seen them?" Crane asked.

"Last known sighting of Plumber was a few days ago, and Lange was seen yesterday. No one has seen either of them since.

And like I said, no one answered last night or now this morning."

"We'll need to find a sympathetic judge," Crane groused.

He thought of Tanner's wife, Federal Judge Sidney Wilcox, but he didn't want to ask for a personal favor. "See what you can do."

"I'll call you back." Crane ended the call.

"I can't imagine a judge will approve a search warrant based on a former association," Morganne protested.

"But there's a compelling argument if you add in the fact that we found Winston's former girlfriend dead and her vehicle missing." He shrugged. "At this point, we don't have any other leads to go on."

She frowned and looked up at the building. From this angle he could see the window of Vince Lange's apartment. So far, there was no indication that anyone was hiding out in there.

His phone rang a few minutes later. "You've got your warrant to search for information related to the whereabouts of Blaine Winston," Crane informed him. "I've sent a copy via email. Don't go off the rails on this, Nelson. You can look at what's in plain sight and talk to the occupants of the apartment, that's it."

"Okay, thanks." Colt pocketed his phone. "Let's go."

He chose Vince's apartment first. The building manager was impressed by the search warrant and readily opened the door. There was no sign of Vince and, unfortunately, no evidence of a crime in plain sight.

"Do you know Mr. Vince Lange?" Morganne asked the manager.

"Not really. He didn't renew his lease—said something about moving to Cheyenne."

Interesting. Colt left the apartment and addressed the manager. "What about Owen Plumber?"

"His lease isn't up for six months yet."

The manager escorted them to Owen's apartment.

There was no evidence of foul play there, either.

"Now what?" Morganne asked, her hands on her hips.

"I don't know." He didn't think heading to Cheyenne without more information to go on would help.

Yet he was just as convinced that Winston had had help in evading them. But who? Vince? Owen?

Or someone else entirely?

NINE

Seeing the two empty apartments was deeply disappointing. Morganne rubbed the knot on the back of her head as she returned to the Jeep. She eyed Colt over the hood of the vehicle. "I'm going to call my boss, ask for a BOLO to be issued for both men."

Colt lifted a brow. "Based on what?"

"They are both persons of interest related to Blaine's whereabouts. We should be able to bring them in for questioning." Like the search warrant, it was a stretch, but she couldn't come up with another idea at the moment.

"Can't hurt," Colt admitted.

She made the call. Lieutenant Graves sounded cranky, but he didn't argue about issuing the BOLOs. After disconnecting, she leaned on the driver's-side door and looked at Colt. "I'm not sure where we should go next."

"When will we have the forensics on the shell casings?"

"I'll call the supervisor." She waited for Andrews to answer. "This is Officer Kimball, following up on the shell casings from the thirty aught six that were found yesterday."

"Oh, yes, Officer, the results just came in. The two shell casings were both ejected from the same rifle, I haven't tested the third one that was just dropped off. If you get me the gun, I should be able to provide a match."

"And no fingerprints, correct?"

"No, sorry."

It was what she'd expected. "What about the hiking-boot print? Do you have a name brand on the shoe?"

"Yeah, we discovered it's a men's size twelve Avalanche low-height hiking shoe.

Relatively common brand available online or at some larger discount stores."

"Okay, thanks." She lowered her phone and frowned at Colt. "Blaine is only five feet ten inches tall, so I find it hard to believe he'd wear a size twelve Avalanche hiking shoe." She paused, then added, "Unless he had to get a bigger size to accommodate a lift. Neal Henderson really stuck to his claim that Blaine was six foot two."

"That only reinforces the possibility he's using a lift in his shoes, and it would explain the height difference." Colt's expression was thoughtful. "Let's check out the stores that sell Avalanche hiking shoes here in the area. Maybe one of the employees will recognize Winston's mug shot."

"Okay." She didn't have a better plan, so she slid behind the wheel and started the Jeep. She headed to the largest store in Jackson, glad to see it was open for business by the time they arrived.

Armed with Blaine's mug shot, they

headed inside. The employees at the two registers were both young women in their early twenties, their name tags identified them as Celia and Noreen.

"Do you recognize this man?" Colt displayed the mug shot.

The girls leaned in to see the photograph better. "He looks vaguely familiar," Celia said with a frown. "He could have been in here."

"Do you work the day shifts often?" Morganne asked.

"Yes, we routinely open the store each day. Dave is the manager. He's around somewhere if you'd like to talk to him."

"We would, yes," Colt said. "Can you remember what this guy might have purchased?"

The two girls looked at each other. "Not really," Celia admitted. "I don't have a clear picture in my mind of him buying anything."

Morganne tried not to show her frustration. It wasn't as if these two young women would have any reason to suspect they were checking out a murderer. "Let's check out the hiking boots," she said in a low voice.

Colt nodded, and they wove their way through the store to the shoe section. The Avalanche hiking shoes were readily available. Colt turned the shoe over and compared the bottom to the picture he'd taken of the tread. "They're a match."

Morganne saw a few shoe inserts, but none that would have added a solid four inches of height. Maybe a half inch at best. Unless he'd doubled or quadrupled them to add more height? Or maybe Neal was wrong.

"Blaine could have purchased the shoes here, but again, no proof of that," she mused.

"Exactly. Celia was far from confident in identifying him." Colt set the shoe down. "I see they sell rifles here, too."

"They would have done a background

check if Blaine had purchased the gun here," she protested.

"If he's using a fake ID, the check would have come back clean," Colt argued. "Let's talk to the manager."

She found Dave in the back of the store talking on his cell phone. When she raised a hand, he quickly ended the call and headed over. "Can I help you with something?"

"Have you seen this man in the store?" Colt held up Blaine's mug shot. "And do you have security video available for us to review?"

Dave peered at the mug shot. "No, I haven't seen him in the store, and I only recognize him from the news. You're welcome to look at my video. I have nothing to hide. Unfortunately, I only keep the video for about a week. My computer doesn't have enough storage to keep it longer."

"A week's worth is great, thanks." Morganne followed Dave into the back room of the store.

Dave bent over the computer keyboard, cued up the video and stepped back. Morganne sat in the chair while Colt leaned over her shoulder. She was far too aware of Colt's closeness, overwhelmed with the memory of their intense kiss.

Concentrating on the screen, they watched the video showing the front door of the store. She fast-forwarded the video when there weren't any people coming or going but slowed it down when customers began to arrive.

It was tedious work, but then again, much of police work was. Morganne planned to take the detective exam the next time it was offered. As much as she wanted to get off routine patrol, she knew being a detective would entail far more paperwork than she dealt with now.

"Stop there," Colt said, his low, husky voice near her ear. "Check out the guy in black."

She paused the video, then backed it up a few frames. She played it in slow motion, peering closely at the man who entered the store. "No, that's not Blaine." She glanced over her shoulder at Colt. "I'm sure I'd recognize him even if he was wearing a disguise."

"Yeah, the nose and mouth are wrong," he agreed. "Okay, keep going."

They stayed in Dave's office for two hours, reviewing the entire week's worth of video, only to come up empty. She rose to her feet and stretched, glancing at Colt. "I guess Blaine could have gotten to town earlier than we anticipated."

"Or he purchased what he needed before coming to Jackson." Colt grimaced. "Which leaves us without any hard evidence to give my boss."

"I know." She made her way back through the store, trying not to feel discouraged. Blaine was a fugitive from the law—surely someone would turn him in eventually.

Her cell phone rang. Upon seeing the lieutenant's number, she braced herself for more bad news. "Kimball."

"The Wyoming State Police picked up Vince Lange for speeding and are bringing him here for questioning. I need you and the marshal to get over here, pronto."

"We'll be there in ten minutes." She slipped her phone in her pocket. "Vince Lange was picked up on the interstate. They're bringing him in so we can talk to him."

"Good. I really hope he turns out to be Winston's accomplice," Colt said grimly. "I want that guy under lock and key."

"I'm with you on that." She tried not to remember the heavy weight of Blaine pressing her to the ground moments before Colt had scared him off.

Once they arrived at the police station, she led the way inside, ignoring the surprised glances that were likely aimed at the fact she was out of uniform.

"Kimball?" She winced at the lieutenant's tone.

"Here, sir." She paused in the doorway of his office. "Where is Vince Lange?"

"Not here yet." Graves waved them both to enter the office. "Tell me you have something on this escaped convict."

Morganne filled him in on what she'd learned from Andrews in forensics.

Jerome Graves scowled and shifted his gaze to Colt. "Can't you come up with the resources we need to find this guy?"

"I'm working on it," Colt said, his tone even. "What about Kay Fisher's murder? Did your guys ever find her boyfriend or the Nissan?"

"The Nissan was found abandoned just outside the Jackson city limits."

Morganne blinked in surprise. "Really? Any prints in the vehicle that we can match to Blaine?"

"The interior was wiped clean, but the tire tread is similar to the one found in the dirt road behind the Wagon Wheel."

Lieutenant Graves's scowl deepened. "And Doug Levine, Kay's boyfriend, was picked up at a local bar late last night, or rather, early this morning. We're waiting for him to sober up before we question him."

"Sounds like it's possible Levine killed Kay," Colt said thoughtfully.

Graves nodded. "Rumor has it that the relationship was rocky, the two of them arguing often, so yeah, it's possible. But the abandoned Nissan Quest wiped clean? That doesn't quite fit the picture."

"No, it doesn't." Personally, Morganne believed Blaine had gone to Kay's house for help. When she didn't agree to offer her assistance voluntarily, he killed her and stole her car. She figured he'd done something similar at his father's trailer.

Apparently those who dared to cross Blaine paid a high price.

Losing their lives.

Colt sensed Morganne's inner turmoil over the lack of progress on their investigation. He glanced at her lieutenant. "Sir, if we can rule Levine out as a suspect, the circumstantial evidence against Winston could be what we need to get those additional resources you asked for," Colt said. "Please keep us posted on how the interview goes and whether or not Levine has an alibi."

"Yeah, yeah." Graves looked as if he hadn't gotten a decent night of sleep since Blaine had been sighted in the area. "We're working on it." His phone rang, and he pounced on it. "Great, bring Lange into interview A."

Colt glanced at Morganne. "Let's have a chat with Winston's former rodeo buddy."

"Maybe he knows where Owen Plumber is, too." Morganne led the way down the hall and opened the door to the interview room.

Vince Lange was dressed in dusty jeans, a Western-style shirt and cowboy boots. He looked at them with apprehension as they stood there. "What's going on? Why am I here? Am I under arrest?" Vince asked.

"You are not under arrest, Mr. Lange. I'm US Deputy Marshal Colt Nelson, and this is Jackson police officer Morganne Kimball. We brought you in because we have a few questions about Blaine Winston."

Vince's eyes widened. "That's what this is about? I haven't seen or heard from the guy since he went to jail for killing those girls."

"He didn't kill me." Morganne stepped forward. "I was the victim that got away."

Vince looked chagrined. "Oh, yeah, I remember now. You brought him down. I'm sure being bested by a woman really stuck in his craw."

Colt moved forward. "Winston is the type to hold a grudge?"

"Oh, yeah." There was no hesitation in the guy's voice. "Big-time. He could get downright obsessive."

Interesting, yet not surprising. "You're

sure he hasn't tried to get in touch with you?"

Vince nodded vigorously. "I'm positive. And you have to know, I wouldn't have helped him if he had. The guy had a reckless streak and a nasty temper. Back then it was easier to be his buddy than to go against him, but now? I'd turn him over in a heartbeat."

"Why are you planning to move to Cheyenne?" Morganne asked.

Vince appeared surprised by the question. "That's where Julie, my fiancée, lives. I just landed a new job with a construction company based there. Driving back and forth between Jackson and Cheyenne has gotten really old."

Colt knew it was at least a six-hour drive one way. "We'd like to talk to your fiancée."

Vince frowned. "But—you're not going to tell her I'm a suspect, are you? I promise I haven't seen Blaine since he was arrested."

"We'll let Julie know you're not a suspect," Morganne assured him. "It's just a formality to confirm your story."

"What about Owen Plumber?" Colt asked. "You guys must be close, as you're living in the same apartment building."

"We're not close." Vince's blunt tone took him by surprise.

"Sounds like you guys had a falling-out," Colt drawled.

Vince flushed. "It's not like we had a big fight or anything. We've just gone our separate ways."

"When's the last time you saw him?" Colt pressed. There was something here that Vince wasn't telling them.

"I—have no idea. I never see him, even less in the past year, as I've been driving back and forth between Jackson and Cheyenne."

"Yet you live in the same apartment building," Morganne said with a smile. "Come on, Vince. You must have run into

Owen at some point. What about the laundry room? Or outside in the parking lot?"

Vince stubbornly shook his head. "I haven't spoken to Owen, and I truly can't tell you the last time I saw him."

Colt glanced at Morganne, wondering what she thought of his comment. She gave a very slight shake of her head, so he remained silent, hoping Vince would break down and tell them whatever he might know.

"I haven't seen him," Vince repeated. "Is that all you want? Can I leave now?"

"Not until we call your fiancée." Morganne leaned closer. "Tell me, does Julie know Owen?"

"No." The denial was swift and forceful. "I'm telling you, Julie lives in Cheyenne and I'm not friends with Owen."

"But you used to be friends." Colt thought he saw a flash of fear in Vince's eyes.

There was another long silence before Vince threw up his hands. "I was the outsider, okay? Owen and Blaine were close, but I was often the odd man out. The two of them weren't always very nice, especially toward women."

Colt pulled out a chair and sat across from Vince. "Tell me more."

Vince licked his lips nervously. "There were always rodeo bunnies. That's what we called girls who were interested in, uh—being with a rodeo star. Owen and Blaine slept around, then dumped them on a regular basis." He flushed. "Listen, I have sisters, and I didn't like the way they treated these girls like they were dirt under their boot heels."

"Were you aware of any physical abuse going on?" Morganne asked.

"No." Vince sighed and rubbed the back of his neck. "But I'll be honest with you, when I heard Blaine attacked and killed those young women, I wasn't that surprised. He had a deep, dark mean streak in him and seemed to have a grudge against women. I'm sorry to say I ignored that streak for years, when I should have known better."

"What about Owen?" Colt asked. "Did he have a similar temperament?"

"Not as much of a temper as Blaine had, yet they were similar in how they treated women." Vince sighed. "At least until Blaine was arrested."

"How exactly did Owen treat women?" Morganne pressed.

Vince lifted his hands. "Other than taking advantage of them? I don't know. I've never seen Owen hurt a woman, if that's what you're asking."

"Where does Owen work?" Morganne asked. "We've been by his apartment a few times, but he hasn't been there."

Now Vince looked annoyed. "I told you, I haven't seen or spoken to him. The last I knew, and that was a few years ago, Owen drove an eighteen-wheeler for work. No clue if he's still trucking or not."

Colt sat back in his seat. If Owen was trucking across country, it would explain why he hadn't been around the apartment for the past few days.

"Do you know anything else that would help us find Owen or Blaine?" Morganne reached across the table to touch Vince's forearm. "It's important. We need to make sure he doesn't hurt or kill another woman."

"I wish I knew something that would help you catch him." There was no mistaking the sincerity in the man's eyes. "I kept my sisters away from him, and it makes me sick to think about how he killed those other girls."

"Okay, then." Morganne released his arm and rose to her feet. "Thanks for coming in to talk to us."

"I wasn't given a choice," Vince pointed out dryly. "But I'm not angry. I totally understand why you brought me in. And if I knew something that would help, I'd tell you."

Morganne pushed a business card across the table at him. "If you think of anything else, please let us know."

"Yeah, sure." Vince looked a bit shell-shocked as he put the card in his pocket.

Colt waited until Vince left, then closed the door behind him. He faced Morganne. "Based on that interview, we really need to find Owen Plumber. Especially since Owen used to drive a semitruck."

"Why is that important?" Morganne asked.

"A semitruck is what slammed into the ambulance carrying Winston to the hospital." Colt's expression was grim. "Sounds to me like Owen might have been his accomplice in escaping nine months ago."

Morganne looked stunned. "I can't imagine that connection wasn't discovered sooner."

Colt understood her disbelief. "The driver was identified as Eli Hornbrook, but I'm wondering now if Eli did the deed as a favor to Owen."

"Maybe. Let's head over to an empty desk and borrow a computer." She moved toward the door. "Sitting on his apartment building is a last resort. If he is helping Blaine, it's not likely he'll be heading there anytime soon. For all we know, Owen is driving Blaine around town as we speak."

"Run his DMV record, find out what car he's using," Colt urged as she dropped into a desk chair and booted up the computer.

A couple of keystrokes later, she gestured to the screen. "A forest green Chevy pickup truck." He quickly wrote down the license plate number. "Let's get a BOLO out on this car."

As Morganne picked up the desk phone and made the call to the dispatcher, Colt found himself wondering about the so-called friendship between Winston and Owen Plumber.

He used his cell phone to make a call of his own. "I need to know if Owen Plumber ever visited Winston in prison."

"I'm not here to be at your beck and call," James Crane groused. "I'm sure all known associates were vetted after the initial jailbreak."

They had, but something must have gotten missed along the way. He thought for a moment. "Let's try a different angle. Did Winston have any visitors with the same initials?"

After more muttering Crane finally answered. "Nope. Just his lawyer, Don Rolland."

"Rolland could have reached out to Owen at some point." The more Colt considered this possibility, the more convinced he was that tracking down Plumber would lead them straight to Winston.

They just had to find him.

TEN

Morganne listened to Colt's side of the conversation with his boss, wondering about Owen Plumber's friendship with Blaine. If Vince was correct in describing their relationship, it seemed logical that Blaine might have sent his lawyer some information to give to Owen, convincing the guy to help him out. Yet if Rolland had done that, he risked losing his law license. And if Blaine had help from Owen, why had he killed Kay Fisher?

There were too many moving pieces to the puzzle. She began typing at the computer, sketching a potential timeline of events. She started with the first sighting of Blaine by Neal Henderson at the Wagon Wheel, then added the crime scenes, including all the various attempts against her.

It was possible Blaine's first stop upon returning to the area had been his father's place in Rock Springs, possibly to get money and a vehicle. Then he'd come to Jackson, maybe stopped for a drink at the Wagon Wheel, before heading over to visit his former girlfriend.

But why go to Kay's house if he had gotten what he needed from Silas's house? And why not go straight to Owen? Unless the guy had been out on the road.

She abruptly straightened and looked at Colt as he pocketed his phone. "What if Blaine took Silas's vehicle, but it died somewhere along the way, so that was why he went to Kay's house to get her Nissan?"

"It's possible," he agreed.

"Let's check the impound lots. Maybe that's why no one has spotted the Impala." She reached for the phone again and called the closest impound lot, owned by a guy named Todd Gibson. "Mr. Gibson? This is Officer Kimball with the Jackson PD. Do you have a Chevy Impala that's been towed in recently?"

"Sure do. Was brought in two nights ago," Gibson agreed. "Why, do you think it was used in a crime?" There was a note of morbid fascination in his tone.

"Possibly. We'll be right over to take a look, thanks." She replaced the receiver and stood. "Silas's car was brought in two days ago and is in the impound lot. I should have thought of looking there earlier. We may have missed some key evidence." She inwardly railed at herself for dropping the lead.

"Morganne, you can't be on top of every single minute detail of this case." Colt rested a hand on her shoulder. "We've been shot at several times, stumbled across Kay Fisher's dead body and have been following up on the shell casings. We've been working hard—finding Silas's car wasn't exactly a priority."

"I know, but still." She wasn't ready to

cut herself any slack over dropping this thread, but she knew based on her estimated timeline that even if they'd found the Chevy earlier, Kay Fisher still would have been murdered. "I just hope there's more evidence in there that will prove Winston used it."

"That would be helpful. But remember, Winston was working here a full day ahead of us," Colt pointed out. "He must have gone to his father's first, then to the Wagon Wheel, then to Kay Fisher's place."

"I know, I drafted a possible timeline." She led the way outside. "Finding Silas's car wouldn't have changed Kay's murder. But being two steps behind Blaine's every move is getting old. We need to find a way to get in front of this, to anticipate what he'll do next or where he'll go." She couldn't hide her frustration.

"We will." Colt gently squeezed her shoulder. "Have faith."

Faith? She frowned. "I don't think God is helping us investigate."

"God gives us strength, intelligence and courage, so yes, I firmly believe He is guiding us through this."

She marveled that Colt spoke with such confidence about his faith. It hadn't occurred to her that God may have provided her the strength and determination to escape Blaine's initial attack five years ago. Was that something her mother would have believed as well?

Maybe.

She shook off the thought and turned to Colt. "We can walk. The impound lot is just a block away."

"That's fine." Colt paused and turned to scan the area. "We just need to stay alert."

"Always." She didn't protest when Colt slid his arm around her waist to keep her close as they headed down the street toward the impound lot. While she told herself Colt's only intent was to keep her safe, there was no denying the tiny thrill of awareness that sparked through her nerve endings at his nearness.

Deep down, she found herself wishing this pretend closeness was for real. But he'd given his heart to Abby and wasn't interested in replacing her.

Something she'd do well to remember.

When they reached the impound lot, the manager, Todd Gibson, escorted them through the crowded parking spaces to the old brown Chevy Impala. "Here you go."

She bent down to peer inside the vehicle. The windows were partially open, and the rank scent of stale cigarette smoke made her wrinkle her nose. "I'm not seeing any obvious bloodstains in the front seat."

Colt was looking in from the other side. "No, although we'll need the crime scene techs to use luminol to make sure Winston didn't attempt to clean up after himself."

She walked back around the car and gestured toward the trunk. "I'll call the crime scene techs to come out and look for evidence. Could be Silas's body was stuffed in there at one point." The thought of her uncle's dire fate made her shiver. Not that she didn't believe her cousin could be so heartless, because she knew he was exactly that.

Heartless.

Blaine was obviously a killer without a conscience, desperate to seek revenge. And it was her job to stop him.

No matter what.

Morganne stepped back from the car and once again called her lieutenant. "Find something?" The frank hope in his tone made her wince.

"Yeah, actually, we have Silas's vehicle in the impound lot. We need it checked for forensic evidence, prints, hair fibers, blood, DNA, etc."

"I'll arrange for that." Lieutenant Graves paused, then said, "We need those extra marshals your buddy keeps promising. I've been able to convince the chief to keep the case with the marshals rather than bringing in the FBI."

"Colt is expecting them to arrive this afternoon. Don't worry, we're hot on Blaine's trail. I'm confident we'll have him in custody very soon."

"I hope so. We don't have enough staff to handle any more dead bodies," he groused before disconnecting from the line.

"Morganne? Check this out." Colt was kneeling beside the Impala's trunk.

She came over to crouch beside him. He had his phone flashlight aimed at a dark spot near the edge of the bumper.

"That looks like blood." She glanced grimly at Colt. "This doesn't look good for finding my uncle alive."

"No, it doesn't." Colt slowly rose to his feet. "There's no stench from the trunk, so it's highly likely Winston dumped his father's body somewhere along the interstate."

She sighed. "Yeah, and if that's the case, it could be weeks, even months before he's found."

If his body is found at all, she silently

added. At this point, she wouldn't put anything past her cousin.

Nothing at all.

Colt watched as a squad car pulled up followed by the familiar faces of the crime scene techs. The pair had been busy over the past forty-eight hours, but so far, they hadn't produced much to show for it.

Not their fault that Winston was cruel and cunning. After all, the escaped convict had recently killed one woman, and likely Silas, too. Colt didn't believe the old man was still alive, at this point he'd only slow Blaine down. Two murders in as many days.

And likely others that they didn't know anything about.

His phone rang, and he grinned when he saw Slade's name on the screen. "Tell me something good."

"We're about an hour away," Slade said. "We figured you're so obsessed with food you'd want to meet us for lunch."

"Good idea. Morganne? Where should we meet Tanner and Slade for lunch?"

She looked thoughtful for a moment. "There's a place called the Bucking Bronc, obviously a draw for the rodeo crowd. We might want to talk to the workers to see if anyone knows Owen."

He liked that idea. "Slade? Look for a place called the Bucking Bronc. We'll meet you there in an hour."

"You and Morganne?" Slade teased.

He felt his cheeks redden and hoped Morganne wouldn't notice. "Yeah, once you get here, we'll fill you in on what we've uncovered in the investigation so far."

"Sounds like a plan. So tell me, is this Morganne of yours pretty?"

"See you soon, Slade." Colt ended the call without answering. Slade and Tanner were both happily married, and they never let an opportunity go by to point out what he was missing by remaining single.

They knew he'd lost his girlfriend to a

violent crime, but he hadn't gone into detail about how much he'd loved Abby and how he'd never gotten over her.

Or so he thought.

Being glued to Morganne's side these past couple of days made him realize he'd rarely thought about his feelings for Abby. Especially when kissing Morganne had elicited a thrilling response he'd never expected. One he'd focused on for far too much time, wishing he could experience it again.

He shouldn't have told her about Abby. Would Morganne welcome another kiss? Or punch him in the nose for his efforts?

There was only one way to find out.

Unfortunately, this wasn't the time or place. But maybe, once they had Blaine in custody, he'd ask her on a real date.

Unless, of course, his boss sent him back to Idaho Falls to pick up the protection detail he'd abandoned in favor of tracking Winston.

The thought was depressing.

"Can you open the trunk for us?" Morganne asked the crime scene tech.

"Sure." The tech used gloved fingers to release the trunk latch from inside the car. The lid sprang open, revealing an empty space.

And a large patch of dark and dried blood.

"Okay, guess we'll be getting a DNA sample on this," the tech said dryly.

"There's blood from Silas Winston's house in Rock Springs that we'd like to match with this," Morganne said, gesturing to the stain. "We have reason to believe the blood is from Silas Winston and that his escaped convict son, Blaine, had something to do with his father's demise. Although," she hastily added, "we don't have a dead body to prove murder."

"This is a small amount of blood, which makes me think the guy must have been dead before being placed inside, and maybe even wrapped in a blanket." The tech's expression was grim. "We'll call Rock Springs to get a sample to match."

"Thanks." Morganne turned toward Colt. "Let's head over to the Bucking Bronc early. It will give us time to question the staff before your marshal buddies arrive."

"Okay." He kept her close to his side as they walked back to the police station, where they'd left her Jeep. "Oh, and I'm fairly certain Tanner and Slade will have an SUV to give us. We should use the new SUV rather than your Jeep. I'm sure Winston knows what type of vehicle you drive."

Morganne nodded but didn't say anything more. He'd halfway expected an argument, especially considering how she'd insisted on staying at her place last night. And how Winston had tried to get to her once again.

The trip to the Bucking Bronc didn't take long. The place was similar to the Wagon Wheel, catering to a cowboy type of crowd.

As he followed Morganne inside, he could easily envision a former rodeo rider like Owen Plumber hanging out there. There weren't many patrons inside despite it being half past the noon hour. It was one of those places that likely saw more action in the late-night hours.

He pulled out his mug shot of Blaine and offered it to the bartender. "I'm US Deputy Marshal Colt Nelson. Can you tell me if you've seen this man recently?"

The potbellied man squinted at the image. "I remember Blaine from years back but haven't seen him since he got himself arrested."

"So you remember Blaine Winston?" Colt was intrigued by his response.

"Sure. All those rodeo guys spent a good portion of their hard-earned money here." The man grinned, revealing nicotine-stained teeth. "Blaine had a reputation for being a bit of a jerk, though."

That was probably putting it mildly, Colt

thought sardonically. "You must know Owen Plumber then, too."

"Yeah, he still shows up here, although not lately." The guy took a rag and wiped the top of the bar, avoiding his direct gaze.

"When was the last time you saw Owen?" Colt pressed.

"I dunno. Maybe a couple weeks ago." The bartender turned his attention to Morganne. "Can I get you two something to drink?"

"No, thank you," Morganne said politely. "We would like to eat lunch, though. A table for four, please."

"Ida May will get you a table." He turned and raised his voice. "Ida? We got customers!"

"Coming, Henry!"

Henry and Ida probably owned the place. Colt stepped closer to the bar. "Sir, I really need to know the last time Owen Plumber was in here."

The older man scowled. "I just told you."

"You should know we could arrest you

for harboring a fugitive," Morganne said, giving him a hard stare. "I'm sure you don't want to end up in jail and leave Ida to run this place on her own."

"What's this about going to jail?" A pear-shaped woman with shoulder-length gray hair hurried forward. "Henry, what did you do now?"

"I didn't do nothin'!" Henry snapped, although he eyed Morganne warily.

"He's withholding information related to a man named Owen Plumber," Colt said. "Do you know him?"

Ida's eyes widened. "Everyone knows Owen. He rambles on and on about the good old days riding broncs." She snorted. "As if anyone cares."

"When's the last time Owen was in here?" Colt asked. When Henry opened his mouth, he put a hand up in warning. "I'm asking Ida, not you."

Ida flushed. "Owen was here three nights ago. Closed the place down, right, Henry?"

"I don't remember." Henry stubbornly stuck to his story.

"You don't want to protect a murderer, Henry." Colt's tone was lined with steel. "And if I find out you helped Winston or Plumber escape, I will arrest you on federal charges of aiding and abetting a known felon, do you understand?"

Henry's cheeks turned beet red, but he gave a curt nod.

"Um, did you say something about a table for four?" Ida asked, breaking the silence.

"Yes, please. We have two more US marshals joining us." Morganne looked directly at Henry as she spoke.

The man muttered something beneath his breath then sighed heavily. "Look, Owen may have been in here three days ago, but I know for sure that Blaine Winston hasn't stepped foot in here. And if he did, I'd call the police."

"Glad to hear that," Colt said with a humorless smile. "Because the man is a ruthless killer, and I'd hate for you or Ida to become his next victims."

Henry paled. "And you think he's working with Owen?"

"Let's just say that Owen is a person of interest in an ongoing investigation," Morganne said.

"Here's my card." Colt placed it on the bar. "I need you to call me if you see Owen."

Henry swallowed hard. "Yeah, sure. I'll do that."

Satisfied they'd gotten their message across to the owners, he and Morganne followed Ida to a booth with windows overlooking the parking lot. He waited for Morganne to slide in first, then took a seat next to her.

"Would you like something to drink?" Ida asked as she placed menus in front of them. "We have soft drinks and lemonade."

"Lemonade sounds good," Morganne said. "Thanks."

"For me, too," he agreed. After Ida left, he lowered his voice so only she could hear him. "Sounds like Owen was here the night before Kay Fisher was murdered."

"Yes, which makes me think Owen was on the road when Blaine got into town. Might be why Blaine was sighted at the Wagon Wheel and ended up going to Kay's house." Morganne frowned. "It fits with the timeline so far."

"Yeah." He hesitated, then added, "I just hope Owen Plumber is still alive, since Blaine seems to be eliminating anyone who might be able to testify against him."

"Or he's only killing those who refuse to help him," Morganne countered. "If Owen is a willing participant and set up the trucking accident to help him escape nine months ago, Blaine might keep him around."

Anything was possible, but based on what had transpired so far, Colt didn't think Owen would be alive for long.

The minute Winston didn't have any use

for the guy, the ruthless killer would get rid of him. The way he had gotten rid of so many others.

Without a flicker of remorse.

"We need to talk to Winston's lawyer, Don Rolland."

"I did a search on him," Morganne admitted. "He's dead. Apparently had a heart attack two months ago."

"After Winston's escape." Colt didn't like it. He glanced out the window, wishing Tanner and Slade would get there already.

"You haven't looked at the menu." Morganne looked up. "I've heard the barbecued ribs are very good here."

"You've never tried them?" Normally, he was all about the food, but for the first time in what seemed like forever, he was distracted by the manhunt and wanting his buddies to get there to help them out.

A flicker of light caught his eye. Colt instinctively yanked Morganne down at the exact same moment that a gunshot rang out, shattering the window into zillions of little pieces that rained down on them.

Winston was out there!

ELEVEN

Morganne crawled beneath the table, shaking the shards of glass from her hair and clothes. She didn't know why she was surprised that Blaine had found her at the Bucking Bronc, but she was.

His constantly showing up and shooting at her was getting mighty tiresome.

She glanced at Colt, who was kneeling on the floor beside her. "We need to head out the back, see if we can find him."

"No, we should wait," he argued. "Give me a minute to call Tanner and Slade. I know they'll be here soon."

"Go ahead and call them, but I'm going out the back." She wasn't asking permission, and she also wasn't going to sit around while Blaine escaped again.

She came out from under the table, remaining in a crouched position, weapon in hand as she darted through the pub. The few customers were all huddled on the floor beneath their respective tables. Henry had ducked down behind the bar, and she assumed Ida was in the kitchen.

She poked her head into the kitchen but didn't see Ida. Rather than searching for the woman, she went out through the rear door of the tavern. Staying close to the wall of the structure, she inched toward the corner. Estimating that Blaine was sitting with his rifle somewhere across from the building, she tried to envision the best hiding spot.

She heard Colt come up beside her. "See anyone?"

"Not yet." She turned to look at him. "What did you see out the window? You yanked me down seconds before the gunfire."

"Sunlight bouncing off a scope." He put a hand on her arm. "I'm thinking he's on the roof of the building across the parking lot."

His observation made sense. But before she could move, Colt put a hand on her arm. She frowned. "What?"

He lifted his phone to his ear. He must have had it on vibrate. "We're pressed up against the back of the tavern," he said in a low voice. "Shooter might be on the roof of the building across the parking lot."

Morganne couldn't hear the response. It was nice to have backup, and she felt certain the Jackson PD would show up any minute, too. Shaking off Colt's hand, she moved forward to peer around the corner of the building.

There was no sign of Blaine. As she watched, two black SUVs drove into the parking lot. She winced, hoping Blaine wouldn't shoot at the marshals. Thankfully, there was no gunfire.

Did that mean Blaine had already escaped?

Without hesitation, she darted around

the corner and ran straight toward the building. Within seconds, she felt Colt coming up behind her.

The building housed a store that sold leather saddles and blankets, along with other horse tack and general rodeo supplies. She burst in and pinned the man behind the counter with a fierce look. “Where is he?”

“Who?” The man’s attempt to sound innocent failed miserably.

“Blaine Winston.” She swept her gaze around the space, looking for a stairwell leading to a second floor.

But she didn’t see anything.

Colt strode over and grabbed the man’s arm, holding his badge inches from his nose. “Tell us where he is or we’ll arrest you for aiding and abetting.”

The guy paled. “I—didn’t do anything. I was in the back room when I heard the doorbell chime. When I came out, there was no one in the shop. It wasn’t until I heard the gunfire that I realized someone must have come inside."

"Where is he?" Colt demanded.

"G-gone. Ran out of here like the place was on fire."

"Where is the stairwell leading up to the second floor?" Morganne asked.

"Through that door." When Colt released him, he came over to open a door that hadn't been visible from where she'd stood.

She hurried past and took the stairs to a small loftlike area. There were several windows that overlooked the parking lot and the entire wall of the Bucking Bronc tavern. The middle window was open, and she could tell it was the vantage point Blaine must have used to fire at her.

Unfortunately, the loft was empty.

Blaine had once again gotten away.

A red-hot ball of fury had her spinning on her heel and thundering back down the stairs to confront the shop owner. "Are you sure you didn't just let him go up there to shoot at me?" she demanded harshly.

"I didn't! I swear on my mother's grave, I didn't know!" The guy backed away with his hands up. "Don't arrest me. I didn't have anything to do with this."

"Did you get a good look at his face?" Colt asked as he pulled Blaine's mug shot from his pocket. "Is this the guy?"

"I—uh, maybe." The man sounded far from certain. "I mean, it could have been him. It all happened so fast."

"Marshal Nelson didn't ask you if it could have been him," Morganne said with restrained frustration. "He asked if you could identify him. That's a yes-or-no answer."

"Y-yes?" The inflection in the man's tone was such that she knew he was telling them what he thought they wanted to hear.

"And you'll testify to that in court?" Colt asked.

He blanched. "Oh, uh, well…no. I didn't get a close enough look at his face."

Morganne blew out a breath and turned away. Clearly the guy wasn't a solid witness. She and Colt might believe the shooter was Blaine—after all, how else would Blaine know about this spot? He must have been a frequent visitor back in his rodeo days.

Unless Owen had told him about it? She quickly turned back to Colt. "Do you have the picture of Owen?"

"I do." Colt pulled it from his pocket and showed it to their reluctant witness. "Does this man look familiar?"

"Well, yeah, I know Owen," the guy admitted.

Her pulse spiked. "Could he have been the one who took the shot at the tavern?"

"No, for sure the shooter wasn't Owen." For the first time since they'd been there, the shop owner spoke with confidence. "I'd have recognized him."

"Okay, thanks." Morganne glanced at

Colt, who gave a subtle nod. They moved toward the door.

"I'm sorry," the shop owner called out as they left.

Morganne looked over her shoulder. "I know, but you need to be careful. That man is armed and dangerous. He's killed before, and he'll do it again."

He blanched. "I understand."

She walked outside and noticed two tall men crossing over to meet them. A wide grin broke out over Colt's features.

"About time you guys got here." He one-arm hugged both of them. "This is Officer Morganne Kimball. Morganne, this is Slade Brooks and Tanner Wilcox."

"Pleasure to meet you, ma'am," Tanner drawled.

"Yeah, we've heard a lot about you," Slade teased.

She inwardly sighed. Just what she needed, to be surrounded by more testosterone. "Nice to meet you. I've heard a lot about the two of you as well."

That caused the two men to look at each other in surprise.

"All good stuff, I'm sure," Slade said with a smile.

"No, most of it was bad stuff," Morganne shot back. "But don't worry, your secrets are safe with me."

The two men gaped at her, and she hid a smile as she turned toward Colt. "Based on the recent gunfire, we might want to find a new place to eat lunch."

"Sounds like a good plan, but we'll have to provide our statements first." Colt nodded at the squad car that pulled up next to the two black SUVs. "Looks like your boss is here."

"Great," Morganne muttered. "Hopefully this won't take long."

Lieutenant Graves scowled when she and Colt approached. "This constant shooting is getting out of hand. Somebody's going to get hurt."

Morganne nodded. "I completely agree. Here's what we know so far." She filled her boss in on the recent events. Inside, she introduced Henry and Ida, who both knew Owen Plumber.

"And you still think your cousin is behind this?" Lieutenant Graves asked.

"Absolutely." She didn't hesitate for a second. "We believe Owen Plumber is helping him. Finding Owen should help us track down Blaine."

"Yeah, if the idiot doesn't get killed first," her boss said on a sigh. The lieutenant surveyed the broken window and the glass shard debris. "That was a close call, Kimball."

She couldn't deny it. "Thanks to Deputy Marshal Nelson's quick reaction, we managed to escape unscathed."

"I have two US marshals waiting for us outside," Colt added. "We're hoping to come up with a plan to find Plumber, who will then lead us to Winston."

"Good." The news perked him up. The lieutenant nodded with relief. "Get to work, then. But keep me posted on your progress." As they turned away, he called out, "Oh, and Kimball?"

She faced him. "Yes?"

"I'm supposed to let you know that Goldberg was released from jail a few days ago, based on some legal technicality."

Morganne's pulse kicked up at the news. "Russ Goldberg is guilty of being a dirty cop."

"I know that," the lieutenant said wearily. "Regardless, there are still charges pending, so he's under house arrest. I just wanted you to know."

"Thanks." Morganne glanced at Colt. His expression was grim, and she knew he was very aware of the dirty cop who'd nearly killed his friends Duncan and Chelsey, who were now married and living in Milwaukee.

Thankfully, she'd listened to her instincts and followed Goldberg that fateful day to prevent that from happening.

"Be safe, Kimball. You, too, Nelson."

"We will, sir." Morganne turned and

headed back outside. There wasn't time to discuss the Goldberg situation, as Slade and Tanner came over to join them.

"We found a place to eat," Slade said, holding up his phone. "Rhonda's Café."

"We've eaten there before. The food is good," Colt said.

"Of course you have," Slade joked. "I'm sure you've eaten at every single restaurant in Jackson by now."

"Pretty much," Colt agreed. "Morganne, we'll need to leave your vehicle here, at least for now. I'm convinced Winston knows what you're driving."

She swallowed a protest. "Okay, fine."

"We brought one of the SUVs for you to use, Colt." Tanner tossed him the keys. "We'll follow you and Morganne to the diner."

Soon the four of them were huddled in a booth at Rhonda's Café. Morganne put the news of Goldberg aside as her stomach rumbled with hunger.

"Do you have the menu memorized,

Colt?" Tanner asked with a grin. "Tell us what's good."

"The butter burger is to die for," Colt said with a straight face.

The two marshals burst out laughing. Morganne found herself joining in.

Maybe it was silly to find release in a pathetic joke, but after being thwarted by Blaine at every turn, she couldn't deny feeling relieved that she and Colt weren't the only ones looking for her cousin.

The sooner they arrested Blaine, the better.

Yet at the same time, she knew it wouldn't be easy to watch Colt depart Jackson, leaving her to return to being a street cop once this nightmare was over.

Colt had proven to be an amazing partner.

One she'd deeply miss when he was gone.

Once they'd ordered their meals, Colt leaned forward and dropped his tone. "Listen, we really need to find a guy by the name of Owen Plumber. We have reason to believe he's the key to finding Winston."

"They were rodeo buddies before Blaine got arrested for killing those women and almost killing me," Morganne added. "Owen was a semitruck driver, and a semi crashed into the ambulance that allowed Blaine to escape nine months ago. The driver wasn't Owen, but we believe he's the key."

"How so?" Tanner asked.

"Blaine's lawyer may have played a part, but we can't question him because he died two months ago," Morganne admitted.

There was a moment of silence as his fellow marshals digested this.

"We're here to help. Crane told us to stick around for as long as you need us," Slade said.

"Yeah, so what's the plan?" Tanner asked.

"I thought maybe you could stake out

Owen's apartment." His suggestion was greeted by matching scowls.

"I doubt the guy is stupid enough to return to his apartment," Tanner said logically. "We need to figure out where they're hanging out between shooting attempts."

His buddy made a good point. He glanced at Morganne. "Any thoughts on that angle?"

She pursed her lips. "I think Silas's place is too far, so that's probably out. Maybe Owen has family in the area." She pulled out her phone. "I'm an idiot for not thinking of that earlier."

"Well, now, cut yourself some slack. The two of you have been running from this guy's attempts to kill you since the beginning," Slade said kindly.

"Yeah, and trust me, we've both been there," Tanner added, jerking his thumb between himself and Slade. "You and Colt are still alive, and that's all that matters."

Colt was glad his buddies had shown

their support. "We will find him and put him away for the rest of his life."

"Hear, hear," Slade said, lifting his water glass in a toast. They all clinked their water glasses together.

"Looks like Owen's parents live in Montana," Morganne said with a sigh. "That's out."

"We'll find him," Colt said encouragingly.

When their meals arrived, Colt bowed his head. Morganne slipped her hand into his beneath the table, and a rush of warmth washed over him. "Dear Lord, we thank You for continuing to keep us safe in Your care. Bless this food we are about to eat, and continue guiding us on Your path. Amen."

"Amen," Slade, Tanner and Morganne echoed. It was a long moment before she released his hand.

"You've been checking Plumber's social media, right?" Tanner asked Morganne.

"Any siblings? A current or former girlfriend, perhaps?"

The girlfriend angle reminded Colt of Kay Fisher. It was disturbing to realize another innocent woman might be in harm's way because of Winston's thirst for revenge.

"I haven't found one yet," Morganne said between bites. She continued scrolling through her phone. "Hey, wait a minute. Here's a picture of a woman standing beside Owen. I think it must be a friend of his. Romantic or strictly friendship, I can't say for sure."

Colt leaned closer to see the image. "Either way, she's a possibility. Can you find out her name?"

"Sally Birch." Morganne's expression turned grim. "We'd better find Sally before it's too late."

"We will." He strove to sound confident. After taking a bite of his butter burger, he called Crane. "I need everything you have on a Sally Birch."

"Okay, okay, give me a minute." There was a long silence before Crane came back on the line. "I've got her address and a description of her car."

"Send them to me," Colt said. "We're heading there as soon as possible." He slipped his phone in his pocket and took another bite of his burger. When the email came in, he scanned it quickly. "Okay, Sally lives in a small house, not far from where Morganne lives, actually." Was that a coincidence? Maybe, as Jackson wasn't that big. He eyed Tanner and Slade. "We should split up and approach her house from the front and the back."

"And pray we find Sally alive and unharmed," Morganne added.

"Yes," he agreed. His buddies nodded solemnly.

They quickly finished their meal and paid the tab. Outside, he pulled up the location of Sally's home on his phone to show the others. "Tanner and Slade, I want you to go up to the front door, because

Winston won't recognize you. Morganne and I will cover the back."

"Sounds like a plan," Tanner drawled.

Colt glanced at Morganne as he drove the short distance to Sally's house. "This is a good lead, Morganne."

"I hope so." Her smile was lopsided. "I really hope she's okay."

He did, too. Driving around the block, he pulled over at the side of the road. "Let's do this."

Weapons held ready, Colt and Morganne took two different paths through the neighbors' yards so they could keep an eye on the back door.

Colt knelt near the base of a tree. Morganne was positioned within view behind a low bush. He watched the back door of Sally's house, hoping they'd catch Winston in the act of fleeing from the scene.

At this point, he'd gladly take Plumber, instead. Anyone with knowledge of Winston's whereabouts would be helpful.

He strained to listen but was too far back

to hear anything going on at the front of the house. Thinking about how Slade and Tanner were both happily married now made him feel a little guilty about dragging them over to help.

Dear Lord, please watch over us all!

The whispered prayer helped steady his nerves. Then he heard the sound of gunfire.

No! He leaped to his feet just as a man came barreling out of the back door of the house, holding a gun. Without hesitation, he lifted his weapon. "US marshal! Drop your gun and put your hands on your head!"

The man didn't listen. Instead the gun swung in Colt's direction. He recognized Owen Plumber the moment before the guy aimed at him and pulled the trigger.

TWELVE

Operating on pure instinct, Morganne fired at the man who ignored the order to drop his gun and who turned to shoot at Colt. The man stumbled backward beneath the force of the bullet. He finally dropped his gun as he fell to the ground.

"Colt!" She didn't dare take her gaze off the gunman as she rushed forward to kick his weapon far out of reach.

"I'm okay." Colt quickly joined her near the fallen man. "Owen? Can you hear me?"

The sense of relief that Colt was unharmed was staggering, but she managed to stay focused on the issue at hand. She knelt at Owen's side, opposite Colt, and gathered up his shirt to press it against the wound in his right upper chest.

"Owen," Colt said loudly. "Where's Blaine Winston?"

The injured man tried to open his eyes, but his gaze wasn't focused. She noticed he was taking rapid shallow breaths and understood he likely had sustained a lung injury.

"Where's Blaine?" Morganne asked, leaning her weight on the wound in an effort to stop the bleeding. "Please, we need to find him."

Owen turned to look at her, his gaze finally beginning to focus. "Ro-rodeo..."

She frowned. "Rodeo? I know you both worked the circuit together. Or are you referring to a restaurant? Or a place? A house?" She could barely contain her frustration. "This will go easier for you if you tell us where we can find Blaine."

Owen didn't respond. His eyelids closed and his face went slack as he lost consciousness.

"Everyone okay?" Slade and Tanner came out through the back door of Sally's house. "We called 911. Ambulance should be here any minute."

"We're good. Did you find anyone else inside?" Colt asked. "Any sign Winston was there?"

"We didn't find Sally or Winston. And no sign of a car for either of them. I can't say if the convict has been there recently or not—we'll need crime scene techs to dust for prints to know for sure," Slade answered. He gazed at the injured man. "I take it this is Owen Plumber?"

"Yeah," Colt said grimly. "And we need him to survive so he can help lead us to Winston."

"I had to shoot him," she said defensively. "He fired his gun at you, Colt."

"I know," he assured her. "I'm not being critical, just don't want to lose our best lead."

She understood what he meant—she wanted to find Blaine as much as Colt did.

Maybe more.

Sirens shrieked as a squad and ambulance approached. Their location in the back of the house made it difficult to see the vehicles, but Slade and Tanner went out front to show the officers and EMTs the way.

Morganne tried not to groan when her lieutenant approached with a scowl on his face. "What on earth happened?"

She continued applying pressure to Owen's wound as the EMTs crouched beside her, rummaging through their supplies. Only when the closest EMT nudged her aside did she relinquish her position. The same female EMT offered her wipes to clean the blood off her hands.

She used them and faced her boss. "US Deputy Marshal Nelson identified himself and instructed Owen Plumber to drop his gun. Owen didn't comply and turned to shoot at Colt. I was forced to shoot him first."

"Owen's bullet grazed my arm," Colt

added. She whipped around to look more closely. Sure enough, his left sleeve was bloody. "Officer Kimball saved my life."

"You told me you weren't hit," she said, moving over to examine his wound more closely.

"It's nothing, just a graze." Colt kept his gaze on her boss. "We wouldn't have shot at Plumber if he'd cooperated with us. We need him to find Winston."

Lieutenant Graves let out an exasperated sigh. "The chief is going to force me to call the FBI for more manpower. We can't keep up with the crime scenes Winston is leaving in his wake."

Morganne bit back a protest, because her boss was right. These attempts against her were over-the-top and unrelenting. Honestly, they needed all the manpower they could get. As things stood, they had too many officers tied up at various crime scenes and not enough out searching for Blaine.

Her boss glanced down at Owen. The

EMTs had placed an IV and were giving fluids as well as packing his wound. The beeping on the heart monitor was somewhat reassuring, and she found herself silently praying that Owen would survive.

She had never killed someone in the line of duty. Not that she wouldn't shoot again under the same circumstances, but she didn't like being in the position of taking a life.

As if sensing her distress, Colt moved closer, taking her hand in his. "He's going to make it."

"I hope so." She glanced again at his wound. "You need the EMTs to take a look at that."

"Who's hurt?" the female EMT asked with a frown.

"This man is more critical." Colt waved his hand toward Owen.

"We have him stabilized," the male EMT said. "We're about to lift him onto the gurney so we can get him to the hospital."

"Let me see your injury." The female EMT stripped off her gloves and donned new ones. She moistened gauze and cleaned Colt's wound. "It's not as bad as the blood made it look, but you probably need to head over to the clinic for antibiotics."

"I will, later." Colt didn't so much as grimace as she took care of his injury.

When the wound was clean, the EMT wrapped fresh gauze around it. "That should hold you until you get to the clinic, but don't wait too long. You don't want to risk the wound getting infected."

"He won't," Morganne assured her as she sent Colt a warning glare. "I'll make sure he goes in."

"Good." The EMT turned back to Owen, helping lift him onto the gurney. Seconds later, they were wheeling him away.

"I'd like to check out the house," Colt said, changing the subject. "Maybe there's something inside that will help us find Winston."

Morganne was on board with that plan. Thankfully, her lieutenant was talking on the phone and didn't notice the four of them going back inside.

"Rodeo," she murmured as she and Colt entered the kitchen area. "Do you think Owen was telling us where Blaine was? Or just how he knew the guy?"

"I wish I knew," Colt said wryly.

She opened drawers, looked into cupboards but didn't find anything remotely useful. They moved into the living room, then upstairs to the bedrooms.

Standing in the hallway, she could see into both bedrooms. "Both beds have been used," she observed. "Could be Blaine was here."

"Or it could mean that Sally made Owen sleep alone," Colt argued. "Especially if they were just friends and not dating."

She hated to admit he was right. The first bedroom revealed nothing of interest. In the second bedroom, there was a matchbook from the Bucking Bronc. "Colt? Come take a look."

He peered over her shoulder at the matchbook. "We already know Owen was a frequent customer there. Could be this was where he was staying."

"Rodeo," she repeated. "Do you think Owen meant the Bucking Bronc?"

"We've already been there," Colt reminded her. "And there wasn't any living space above the restaurant and bar."

"Maybe he was trying to tell us that Blaine was the one who took the shot at us from the rodeo store," she mused. "Or maybe the store owner lied to us and Blaine was living in that loft space. Although I didn't see a sleeping bag or anything to indicate that."

"Let's go," Colt said, waving toward the steps leading to the main level. "We need to meet with Tanner and Slade to figure out our next move."

She nodded and led the way downstairs. Glancing at her bloodstained shirt made her grimace. “My house is three blocks away. Let’s stop there for a minute so I can get a change of clothes.”

“I have a spare shirt for you, Colt,” Slade offered. “I think stopping at Morganne’s place is a good idea.”

“Hey! Where do you think you’re going?” Lieutenant Graves asked, coming up to stand in front of them.

“We need to keep searching for Blaine,” Morganne said.

“You know the rule, Kimball. All officers in a shooting need to be placed on administrative leave,” he protested.

“Under normal circumstances, yes,” Morganne replied. “But you said yourself, sir, that we’re undermanned. I have Colt as a witness the shooting was justified. He was injured by Owen’s gunfire. If you take me off this case, Blaine could escape, wait a month, then return. I’m respectfully asking that you waive the mandatory administrative suspension due to exigent circumstances.”

There was a long moment of silence as her boss digested this. Finally he nodded. "Fine. Consider your suspension waived. But we need results, and soon, or neither one of us will have a job."

"Yes, sir."

"Oh, one more thing," Lieutenant Graves said. "We finally interviewed Kay Fisher's boyfriend, Doug Levine. Once he'd sobered up, he informed us he had an alibi for the time frame of Kay's murder that has checked out so far. He's still on the suspect list, but frankly it's looking more like your cousin is the one responsible for her death."

She winced, hating the reminder that she and Blaine were related, and watched as her boss stomped off.

"We need to get out of here before he changes his mind." Colt placed a hand at the small of her back.

The four of them headed to their respective SUVs, one in the back of the house and one out front. Colt texted Slade directions, and less than five minutes later, they met up again in her driveway.

"This is where it all started?" Tanner asked, sweeping his gaze over the area. "Winston's first attempt to shoot you?"

"Yeah." She unlocked the front door and was immediately hit by a terrible smell. She instinctively reared back, barreling into Colt, who was behind her.

"Stay back," Colt said, drawing his weapon. "Slade and Tanner, we need to clear the house and the property."

"I'll help you clear the house," Morganne said curtly. "Slade and Tanner can go around back. Just be careful. Blaine has taken refuge in the woods along the rear of the property before."

The two marshals nodded and moved away. She and Colt cleared the living room and kitchen, then moved to the bedrooms, each taking one. When she entered her bedroom, she stopped abruptly, the smell hitting hard as she saw the body lying on her bed.

Her uncle, Silas Winston. And written in blood above the headboard were the words *You're next.*

Hearing Morganne's muffled cry, Colt raced over from the second bedroom she used as an office. When he saw the dead body on her bed and the bloody message written on the wall above it, the tiny hairs on the back of his neck rose in alarm.

Winston was taking a huge risk by coming here and taunting her like this. Yet the grisly scene was worse than any horror flick.

"Come with me." Colt gently guided Morganne from the room, taking her outside. He didn't think Winston was nearby, but he was glad Tanner and Slade were sweeping the property, just in case.

"I can't believe he was in my house, in my bedroom," Morganne whispered hoarsely. "And that he left my uncle's body for us to find."

"I know." He pulled her into his arms and held her close. "I'm sorry."

She leaned against him, resting her forehead against his chest. "Why can't we find him?"

Colt wished he had a good answer, because there was no denying chasing Winston was beyond frustrating. "We will. We have Owen, so he doesn't have his help any longer. And Winston is making a mistake taunting you like this." Only a truly evil, cold-blooded murderer could kill his father and carry him across the state to dump him for them to find.

For a long moment she didn't say anything, then she lifted her head and looked up at him. "You know Blaine won't rest until I'm dead."

"We'll get him." Colt hated seeing the weary desolation in her pretty gray eyes. "Have faith in God, Morganne. In us. We're smarter than he is."

A reluctant smile tugged at the corner of her mouth. "I'd like to think so."

"Believe it." He tucked a strand of her red hair behind her ear, then lightly brushed his thumb over her cheek. "I won't let him hurt you."

Her gaze clung poignantly to his. Colt's heart melted, and he gave in to the need to kiss her.

As before, he was swept away by the sweetness of her kiss. By the rush of emotion that washed over him. It had been so long since he'd experienced this level of attraction, and he found himself wishing he'd never have to let her go.

"Ah, Colt?" Slade's voice splashed over them like a bucket of cold water.

He lifted his head and scowled at his buddy. Morganne hastily stepped back, her cheeks bright pink with embarrassment.

"What?" Colt knew he sounded testy, but surely whatever these guys had found could have waited another minute.

Or ten.

"Sorry to interrupt, but we found hiking-boot prints out back." The wide grin on Slade's face made Colt groan inwardly.

"We've found several of those ourselves," Colt said, reluctantly releasing Morganne. "And by the way, we found the dead body of Silas Winston in Morganne's room and a message written in blood on the wall."

All hint of humor faded from Slade's expression. "You're not kidding."

"No." Colt jerked his thumb toward the front door. "Check it out for yourself."

Slade hurried inside, returning five minutes later with a pale face. "I have a bad feeling this guy is losing his grip on reality."

"He seems unstable for sure," Colt agreed. "And we'll need to call this in."

Morganne closed her eyes. "Lieutenant Graves is going to have a heart attack if we put any more pressure on him."

"Maybe we call our boss and have him send in a few techs," Slade suggested. "I agree with Morganne. There's no way the locals can handle this. Especially if you believe Winston brought the body here from Rock Springs. He must have stored the body someplace in the past few days, too."

Colt didn't have to think twice. "Let's do it."

Tanner joined them in front of the house. Slade made the call while Colt showed Tanner what had been left inside Morganne's room.

"I need a T-shirt," Morganne said, coming up behind them.

"You can't take anything from your room," Colt cautioned. "Not until the crime scene techs have released it."

"Right." She grimaced. "I think I left a load of clothes in the dryer." She turned and headed to the small laundry room off the kitchen, closing the door behind her. Colt and Tanner went outside while she changed quickly.

"Crane is sending two techs," Slade informed them. "He's thinking we may need to add more deputies, too. Even though we don't really have proof Winston is here, his father's body is enough to act on."

"Okay, but we still don't know where he is," Colt said. He glanced up as Morganne emerged from the house. "When we asked Owen where Winston was, he uttered the word *rodeo*."

Tanner frowned. "You mean, like a place? Is there a rodeo going on nearby?"

"There's always a rodeo on weekends starting in May and going through the summer months," Morganne said. "But it's not like Blaine could stay there and hide. It's full of people—someone would recognize him."

"And we were already at the Bucking Bronc and the rodeo supply store," Colt added. "Although maybe we should head back to the store. I'm not convinced that guy gave us the true story about how someone sneaked in when his back was turned."

"Sounds very suspicious if you ask me," Slade agreed.

"Wait a minute." Morganne snapped her fingers and reached for her phone. "There's a Rodeo Rider Road near the mountains. Those of us who are local normally refer to it as the Triple R, which is why I didn't think of it right away."

"Owen used the word *rodeo* in reference to a street?" He moved closer to peer at her screen. "That may not help if there are several houses located there. We have no way of knowing which one he might be hiding in."

"That's just it—there aren't a lot of houses there. It's a long, winding road leading around the base of the mountain." She glanced up at him. "I think Owen was trying to tell us that Blaine is hiding out in the mountains."

"But he's been all around town, shooting and leaving dead bodies. I can't imagine he goes all the way back to the mountains for cover between each attack."

"It's not like Jackson is that big," Morganne countered. Her gaze was riveted to her phone. Using her fingers, she broadened the map of the road. "And there's an abandoned mine in that area. One of the old gold mines from years ago."

"A mine?" He hadn't anticipated that. Glancing at Tanner and Slade, he asked, "What do you think?"

"We head to the mine," Slade said without hesitation. "Try to verify he's there."

"As long as we don't spook him into running," Morganne cautioned. "We need to watch the place from a distance."

Colt nodded slowly. "We need proper gear—vests, long-range weapons, night-vision goggles and a couple of flash-bangs in case we need to force him out of hiding."

"I'll call Crane," Slade said.

Colt glanced at Morganne, marveling at the sheer determination in her clear gray eyes.

It made him want to kiss her again. She was the strongest woman he'd ever known.

And he had no idea how he'd find the strength to leave her once this was over.

THIRTEEN

A rush of adrenaline hit hard. Morganne felt certain Blaine was hiding out in the abandoned mine. In fact, she felt like a complete idiot for not considering that possibility sooner. Looking back at how he'd come and gone throughout town—killing Kay, shooting at them from various locations, while using different vehicles—explained a lot.

He didn't need a house to stay in if he was going back and forth from the mine.

Yet staking out the abandoned mine presented several challenges. The biggest being that it was highly likely there was more than one way in and out of the place. And she had no clue where the exit might be located. If they watched the front and he somehow got away through the back, they'd lose him.

She couldn't bear the thought of Blaine escaping again.

"Okay, Crane wants us to verify Winston is there before sending reinforcements," Slade said. "Although he's getting us the supplies we need. In the meantime, we should try to get eyes on the place. Morganne, what's the best way to approach the mine?"

"There's a dirt road off the Triple R that goes up to the mine, but there should be a chain across it to keep people out." She thought back to the last time she'd seen the actual entryway. Their patrols were limited to making sure the chain was intact, and that was only when they had time.

Which they hadn't had recently.

"What about a spot we can use that's farther away?" Colt asked. "Something similar to that rock where we found the shell casing?"

"That rock is on the opposite side of

where the mine shaft entrance is located." She frowned. "Although it could be close to a tunnel exiting the mine."

"That would explain how Winston found it," Colt said with a gleam in his eye. "I think you're onto something, Morganne."

"Maybe, but keep in mind, Blaine lived in Jackson for a while as well, so he could have stumbled over that rock outcropping at any time." She didn't want them to jump to conclusions, especially if the exit was located somewhere else entirely. "It's a possibility we should check out."

"Okay, Slade, how long before we get our supplies?" Colt asked.

The dark-haired marshal grinned. "He's sending them via prop plane from Cheyenne. We'll have them within two hours."

"Okay, let's find a hotel near the mountains to use as a temporary headquarters," Colt said. "We can plan our strategy while we wait for the supplies."

"We can try the Mountain View Motel,"

she told them. "It's the closest motel to Rodeo Rider Road."

"Works for me," Colt said. "Let's go."

"Shouldn't we wait for the crime scene techs?" Morganne reminded him.

Colt flushed. "Yeah, forgot about that."

"They're coming on the plane," Tanner pointed out. "Morganne, can you get a local cop to hang out here? We only need a couple of hours."

She grimaced and reached for her phone. "Lieutenant? We have another crime scene—a dead body was left at my place. The Feds are sending in reinforcements, but we need an officer to sit on the place until they arrive."

"I can't believe this," her boss muttered.

"Listen, we have a possible lead on Blaine." She hoped the news would alleviate some of her boss's stress. "If this pans out, we'll have him in custody before morning."

"Okay, okay. I'll send a rookie." Graves disconnected from the call.

The rookie was Officer Gwen Turkow. Morganne had been mentoring her a bit, as there were not many female cops on the Jackson PD.

"Hey," Gwen greeted her with a wry grin. "Guess I'm here to babysit."

"You should be aware we believe Blaine Winston did this, and he's armed and dangerous." Morganne didn't want Gwen to treat this assignment lightly. "Watch your back, Gwen."

Gwen straightened and nodded. "Will do."

Satisfied the rookie would do her best, Morganne crossed over to the SUV where Colt and the others were waiting. As Colt drove, her thoughts whirled. Between the four of them, they could cover the front and the rear exits of the mine.

If they knew for certain where the exit was located.

And what if there was more than one?

Unfortunately, she didn't know of anyone who had any sort of map of the mine.

Not when it had been closed down for nearly sixty years.

"Turn left," she said. "In five miles, you're going to hang a right, and the Mountain View Motel should be a half mile up on the left."

"Got it." Colt glanced at her. "I have a good feeling about this. We're going to get him."

"I hope so." She smiled, feeling cautiously optimistic. "I'm just worried there could be more than one exit from the mine."

"There may be, but if we can prove he's there, we'll get enough manpower to cover any and all possibilities," Colt said. "We can even bring in a chopper if needed."

"That would help." She glanced at him, trying not to remember the power of his kiss. Seeing her uncle's dead body had been difficult, especially knowing Blaine had done such a terrible thing to his own father. Somehow, leaning on Colt, being held in his arms and absorbing his strength, hadn't made her feel less of a cop. It had been a long time since anyone had cared about her, as a cop and a woman.

Ironically, Colt's protective and caring attitude didn't bother her any longer.

In fact, she plain and simply liked Colt. More than liked him.

But that was skating on dangerous ground.

"Is that the place?" he asked, interrupting her thoughts.

"Yes." She pulled herself together. They needed to stay focused if they were to succeed in finding Blaine.

"Glad to see the vacancy light is on," Colt said with a wry grin. "At least we know one room is available."

She nodded. "One room is all we need. We won't be sleeping anytime soon. Especially if we find Blaine hiding in the mine."

"Very true." Colt pulled into the parking lot and waited for Slade and Tanner to pull up next to him. "Do you think it's worth asking the motel clerk if he recognizes Winston from his mug shot?"

"Can't hurt, although a motel isn't going to give out a room to a known killer. Not with tourist season right around the corner."

"Being this close to the mine, I figure it's worth a try." Colt slid out from behind the wheel.

Morganne joined the three marshals, heading into the lobby. When they displayed their badges, the young female clerk almost fell over herself to give them two connecting rooms.

"Have you seen this man recently?" Colt held up Blaine's mug shot.

"Only on the news," she admitted. Her eyes widened, and her voice rose in a squeak. "You don't think he's here?"

"No, we don't," Morganne assured her. "We're just covering all bases."

"I—I'll make a copy of that and post it

behind the counter if you think that will help," the clerk offered.

"That would be great, thanks." Colt smiled, and the young clerk batted her eyes at him before turning away with the photo to make a copy.

It occurred to Morganne that Colt didn't seem to be aware of the girl's response to his smile. Many of the guys in town were all too aware of their good looks.

But she didn't get that vibe off any of the three marshals. Granted, both Tanner and Slade wore wedding rings, but somehow she had the impression they'd never worried too much about their looks. They were self-assured and confident in their roles as US marshals.

Just one more thing to admire about Colt. As if there weren't plenty of other traits to like about him. Too bad he was still hung up on his former, and tragically dead, girlfriend.

"Here you go." The young clerk smiled brightly at Colt. "My name is Tiffany.

Please let me know if you need anything. I'm here until five."

"Thanks, Tiffany." Colt took the photo and the room keys. "Be sure to call 911 if you spot that suspect."

"I will," Tiffany called out as they left.

Morganne rolled her eyes, and Slade chuckled. "It's the badge," he said in a conciliatory tone. "Makes them starstruck."

"Huh?" Colt looked confused. "What are you talking about?"

"Nothing," Morganne and Slade said at the same time.

Colt unlocked the doors to each room, and they quickly hauled in the few supplies they had on hand. Mainly their handguns, several rounds of ammo and one measly pair of binoculars.

"I should have grabbed another pair," Tanner muttered.

"Plenty more are on the way." Colt shrugged and pulled several chairs together to form a circle around the small table. "Now, let's try to come up with a reasonable game plan."

Morganne sketched a rudimentary map, including the road that should be blocked off and the general location of the entry to the mine. "There should be two-by-fours nailed across the mine entrance, with a large sign telling people to keep out. But we generally don't go all the way up there to look, unless we hear rumblings of kids trying to get in."

"I imagine that happens fairly often," Colt said with a frown.

"Not since a seventeen-year-old boy almost died in there." Morganne met his gaze. "The thrill of trying to get in waned a bit after a portion of the tunnel wall caved in. The locals are smart enough to stay far away. It's the tourists that are the bigger problem."

There was a moment of silence as the three marshals digested that information.

Reading their somber expressions, she understood what they were thinking—

if they had to chase Blaine through the mine, it was entirely possible they could find themselves suffering a similar fate.

Their best way to survive this was to get Blaine to come out of the mine.

And setting herself up as bait to draw him out might be the best way to accomplish their goal.

Ninety minutes after getting into the motel, they had the supplies they'd asked for. On the way to the airport hangar, Morganne made Colt stop at the clinic for antibiotics. When they returned, they spread out the rifles and loaded them with ammo, then pulled on their vests. Colt made sure Morganne's fit snugly before donning his own.

"They sent six flash-bangs," Tanner said with admiration. "Should be more than enough."

"Yeah, although we need to do a bit of recon before we use them." Colt handed out the binoculars, which were equipped with night-vision lenses and GPS tracking devices. The last thing they needed was to get lost in the mountains. "There are several state police officers along with another pair of marshals on standby once we confirm Winston's location with a visual."

"Let's hit the road." Slade looked eager to go. "It's been a while since I've been in the field."

"Why is that?" Morganne asked.

Slade's smile widened. "I took a less dangerous role after meeting my wife, Robyn. We just found out she's expecting."

"A baby? Really? Congrats!" Colt slapped his buddy on the shoulder, then frowned. "You should have said something. I could have found someone else to help."

"What, and miss all the fun?" Slade shook his head. "We got this. Winston is no match for us."

Colt appreciated his buddy's attitude, but he still didn't like hearing the soon-to-be father would be in harm's way.

He glanced at Tanner, who shrugged. "I agree with Slade. We've got this."

It was too late to do anything now, despite that fact that both of his buddies were now fathers. He blew out a sigh. "Okay. We're going to drive part of the way, then spread out and go in on foot."

"I think we should check out the area around the rock, too," Morganne said. "Maybe we'll be able to spot an exit point of the mine with the binocs."

"We will, but let's look for signs Winston has been there first." Colt led the way outside to the SUVs. They'd decided to take two vehicles, just in case something happened to one of them. "We need to move slowly and methodically. If he's here, we can't afford to make a mess of this."

"Agreed." Morganne had that determined look in her eye again.

Colt drove to the designated spot, pulling off the road and parking. Tanner and Slade stayed back at least forty yards and did the same.

Armed and ready, they split up, heading in two different directions on either side of the road leading to the mine.

Colt was glad Morganne was with him. After hiking close to fifteen minutes, moving quietly through the woods, she held up a hand and lifted the binocs to her eyes.

"What is it?" he whispered.

She didn't respond for several minutes, then lowered the glasses. "The chain that is supposed to be across the road has been taken down."

Colt nodded. "Winston would need to take down the chain if he was driving in and out of the mine."

"Yeah." Morganne tucked the glasses away. "Let's hope we find a vehicle there."

Colt followed her through the woods, glancing up frequently for anything that could be used as a vantage point. They knew from experience Winston would climb trees if needed, and being higher up would give them a better view of the entrance to the mine.

He kept in touch with Slade and Tanner through text messages, including Morganne. They hiked for nearly twenty minutes before stopping.

Once again, Morganne lifted the binocs to her eyes. Colt did the same, scanning the area in an attempt to locate what she was looking at.

"I can see a small part of the mine entrance," she said, excitement in her tone. "But it's still about a hundred yards away."

It took a moment for him to pick it out. From this distance and angle, it was difficult to tell if the boards were still covering the mine entrance or if they'd been removed.

"No sign of a vehicle, though." He lowered the glasses. "Let's keep moving."

Again, Morganne led the way. Colt used his GPS tracker to monitor their progress. The foliage was thick, slowing their pace, but he was glad to have cover.

He lifted his eyes upward, sending up a

silent prayer that God would lead them to Winston and keep them safe.

A large tree up ahead caught his eye. It had thick branches that appeared sturdy enough to hold a man's weight.

Morganne stopped again after thirty yards and used her binoculars to locate the mine entrance. He did the same.

"The boards are gone," she said in a low whisper.

"I see that." A thrill of anticipation washed over him. They were so close to apprehending Winston. "We need to move quieter now, in case he's there."

Morganne nodded. "I still can't see a vehicle."

"I know. Let me check with Tanner and Slade." He shot off a quick text. A minute later, Tanner replied. He suppressed a sigh. "They haven't seen anything yet, either, but are trying to get closer."

"Okay." Morganne was beginning to look dejected, as if this lead wasn't going to give them the results they desperately needed.

They continued making their way through the woods. The terrain was rising now, and they were both breathing hard by the time they reached their next stop.

Through the binocs he could see the entry to the mine was closer now. Yet the Keep Out sign wasn't in view. He imagined it was lying on the ground, near the two-by-fours Winston had likely removed.

But with all the foliage it was difficult to get a decent view. He lowered the glasses and leaned closer to Morganne. They were close enough to the mine that he didn't want to be overheard.

"See that tree?" Colt gestured to the large oak. "I'd like to get up there."

She eyed the wide trunk. "Good idea. I don't think I'm tall enough, but I'll give you a leg up."

They headed over. Colt set his rifle aside, and Morganne laced her hands together to make a sling for his foot. He was amazed by her strength when she heaved him upward with a muffled grunt. He latched onto the lowest branch and hung there for a moment before slowly pulling himself up, ignoring the pain in his injured arm.

Sweat dripped down the side of his face, and he could imagine the dirt and dust getting into his wound. Good thing he'd given in to Morganne's persistent badgering and stopped for the stupid antibiotics while they'd waited for their supplies.

When he was in a good position, tucked in the deep V between two branches, he lifted the binocs. From here, he could easily see the area outside the mine entrance. He took his time, looking all around the dark entrance, searching for movement. He really wanted to get eyes on Winston.

But after what seemed like forever, he didn't see anything.

He lowered the glasses and wiped the sweat from his brow. Winston had to be there. It was the only theory that made sense. Colt lifted the binocs and broadened his search, moving the glasses slowly around the cleared area in front of the mine.

And there it was. His pulse spiked as he spied a dark green pickup truck. The same make and model that had been registered to Owen Plumber.

They'd finally found their escaped convict!

FOURTEEN

Morganne stayed on the ground beneath Colt, unable to see much of anything through the trees and brush. When the branches overhead shook, she lowered her binocs and glanced up.

"Coming down," he whispered.

She moved out of the way, watching as Colt swung with athletic grace and dropped silently to the ground. His gaze was bright with satisfaction, and she hurried over.

"You saw Blaine?"

"No, but Owen's dark green pickup truck is parked about twenty yards from the mine entrance." He reached for his rifle, slinging it over his shoulder.

She sucked in a quick breath. "We found him."

"We did. Owen told us about Rodeo Rider Road, and Owen's truck being parked this close to the mine can't be a coincidence." She watched as Colt pulled out his phone and texted Tanner and Slade.

Morganne couldn't believe they'd finally found him. But the fact that he was likely in the mine didn't mean apprehending him would be easy.

Quite the opposite. Blaine had been using the mine as a hiding spot for the past few days, maybe longer—he likely knew more about the tunnels inside than they did. Especially where the exits might be located. Still, this was the closest they'd come to finding him, and she found herself praying he wouldn't get away. She turned to Colt. "We'll need those additional resources to help grab him."

"I'm on it." Colt was working his phone. "I'm wondering if we should check out the rock area where we found the shell casing, see if we can find an exit nearby."

"I can do that," she offered. "We need someone to stay here to keep an eye on the entrance, in case Blaine decides to leave."

"It would be better if he did." Colt looked up from his phone. "Easier to grab him when he's outside the mine. I'd like to go with you. We can leave Slade and Tanner here to watch the front entrance."

"You can't see the truck from the ground," she pointed out. "The only way to keep a visual on it is from the tree. And I'm not tall enough to take the position myself. Besides, I'm a trained police officer and know the area better than the three of you. I'll be fine."

"Hold on a minute." He was texting again. "Tanner is already on his way."

She suppressed a sigh. "You're not thinking this through, Colt. We need one person to head out to meet up with the additional state police officers. No way will they be able to find this place without help. We need to divide and conquer. Why not give me some time to check the place out? We're burning daylight, and it will be easier to find the exit now than later."

Colt scowled. "What if Winston happens to come out of the exit? You'd be vulnerable, especially as you're his main target in all of this. I'm coming with you, end of discussion."

She narrowed her gaze. So much for his treating her as an equal partner.

Before she could say anything more, a slight rustling of leaves caught her attention. She whirled around in time to see Tanner emerge from the thicket.

"Slade found a position on the other side where he can watch the entrance," Tanner said in a whisper. "I can head up into the tree."

"Thanks. Hopefully this won't take too long." Colt laced his fingers and hefted Tanner up. Then he lifted the rifle up, too. Tanner grabbed it and settled into the same V between branches Colt had used.

"Stay in touch," Tanner said, his low voice wafting softly down to them.

"Will do," Colt promised.

She tried to squelch her irritation as she turned and retraced their steps through the woods. It hurt that Colt didn't believe in her. Especially after she'd proven herself competent more than once since they'd begun this search for her cousin.

Whatever. She shook it off and concentrated on getting out of the woods. Even though they suspected Blaine was in the mine, she continued moving as silently as possible. There was no way of knowing if Blaine had come out of the mine and was also walking through the woods.

At this point, she wouldn't put anything past Blaine. He'd turned into a monster, one she didn't recognize at all from their childhood.

She swallowed hard and kept moving. The hike was easier going down, but it was only a matter of time before they'd be heading up a steep incline to reach the rock.

They rested near Rodeo Rider Road, drinking water from canteens that dangled from their belts. Colt reached out to touch her arm. "Don't be angry with me. I can't help feeling protective toward you."

"I just wish you trusted me."

"I do trust you. I know you'll always have my back, the same way I'll have yours." His green eyes begged her to understand. "This isn't some average killer we're trying to arrest. Winston has a personal vendetta against you. And if I was his target, I have a feeling you'd insist on coming along, too."

She opened her mouth to argue but then closed it. Shame washed over her, because he was right. If this was someone who'd been personally attacking Colt, she would insist on accompanying him. And it was only her complex feelings toward Colt that sent her down the path of resentment.

"I'm sorry." She offered a wan smile.

"I'm tired and crabby, neither of which is your fault."

"Hey, I get it." Colt's grin warmed her heart. "But we're close, Morganne. We'll have him in custody soon. God is guiding us."

She nodded. "I know. Let's keep going, see if we can find the exit before dusk."

"We only have about an hour or so," Colt cautioned. "We need time to get back here and create a plan to surround the mine to flush him out."

"Got it." She pushed to her feet. "We can drive part of the way to save time."

The trip to the rock took almost twenty minutes. As before, they approached as quietly as possible, just in case Blaine was nearby.

"We need to split up to cover more ground," she whispered.

Colt nodded and gestured to the side of the rock closest to the mine entrance. "I'll head this way."

He was being protective again, but she

didn't protest. Just because the one side of the rock was closer to the mine entrance didn't mean the exit was on that side.

The terrain wasn't nearly as wooded here, and that made it easier to look for small or narrow openings in the mountainside. She found two shallow crevasses, neither appearing to be an exit from the mine.

Stubbornly, she pressed on, widening her search area. But she still came up empty.

Battling a wave of discouragement, she lifted her phone just as Colt texted her.

Nothing so far. Ten minutes until we head back.

She replied with a quick okay.

Turning, she made her way back toward the rock Blaine had used as a vantage point to shoot at their SUV, causing them to careen off the road. She'd been so certain the mine exit would be nearby.

A boot print near a scrubby bush caught her eye. She stopped and bent down to examine it more closely. The toe of the boot was pointed toward the rock.

She glanced back over her shoulder, surveying the area. Had she missed something? Or was this simply a case of Blaine walking around before finding the rock?

After searching a bit longer, she still didn't find the exit. The sun hovered on the horizon, and she knew there wasn't time to keep searching, even though one of the mine exits had to be around somewhere.

With reluctance, she returned to meet Colt. The discouragement in his eyes mirrored her own. "I found another hiking-boot print back there, but no sign of the mine exit."

He grimaced. "We'll make sure some officers are stationed in this area, just in case. But for now, we need to get back to relieve Tanner and Slade."

"No sign of Blaine yet?"

He shook his head. "Nope. I have to think he's waiting for dusk to move, so we need to get our team in position ASAP."

"I couldn't agree more." This was definitely the time for action. To surround Blaine and find a way to trap him.

Deep down, she knew her cousin wouldn't go down without a fight, making sure to take as many of them out along the way.

Lord, please keep us all safe in Your care.

Colt ignored the rumbling in his stomach as they returned to the rendezvous point near the tree where they'd left Tanner. They'd eaten a late lunch, but of course it was past dinnertime. Capturing Winston was far more important than food, so he focused on the task before them.

He texted Slade, instructing him to continue watching the mine, then gestured for Tanner to come down from his perch in the tree.

"I think we're going to need a chopper

on standby," he said. "We didn't find the mine exit, so we'll need to use our manpower to cast a wide net around the mine entrance."

"And there could be more than one exit," Morganne pointed out.

"I know." Colt hated to think of the multiple possibilities Winston might have to escape. "The way he's chosen his position in the mountainside will make grabbing him difficult."

"Do you think he knows we're out here?" Tanner asked.

Colt glanced at Morganne, who shrugged. "All we can go by is the fact we haven't seen him outside the mine," she said calmly. "He could be hiding in the woods nearby, but if that's the case, I think we'd have heard him or seen a sign of him. And if he's out in the wilderness, we really need to pull in those reinforcements as soon as possible."

"They're on the way," Colt said. "You and I will need to head over to meet with them. You know the area better, so your input would be helpful as we deploy them to their respective locations."

"I'm happy to oblige." She took several nutrition bars from her pack. "We're not getting dinner anytime soon, so here." She handed them to him and Tanner, keeping one for herself. "It's going to be a long night and we'll need the protein."

"She knows you pretty well, Colt," Tanner teased.

"I have one for Slade, too, but he'll have to wait." She took a bite of her bar. "Once the rest of the officers arrive, are you planning to use the flash-bangs to flush him out of hiding?"

"Yeah, unless you have a better idea." Colt gratefully ate his bar, touched that Morganne had thought of him.

"The risk is that flash-bangs will send him farther into the mine." She grimaced and quickly finished her bar. "Unfortunately, I don't have a better idea. Attempting to sneak into the cave to corner him is a huge risk, too. He'd have the advantage while we'd be going in blind."

That was the same conclusion Colt had come to. "Okay, so flash-bangs to draw him out. A wide circle of officers surrounding the mine to try to grab him if he flees. A chopper overhead can help us search." He looked at Tanner, then Morganne. "What am I forgetting?"

"One of us should stay up in the tree," Tanner said. "If he runs out of the mine, the spotter can follow his path, alerting the others."

"Good idea. I nominate you as the spotter," Colt said with a grin.

"Gee, thanks," Tanner responded dryly. "I was hoping you'd take that boring job."

"No way, it's all yours." Colt would rather have had Tanner on the ground covering the perimeter, but he figured the guy would be safer perched in the tree. Tanner was a father to Sidney's adopted daughter, Lilly, and Slade had a pregnant wife. He wanted both family men to be on the outskirts of the action if at all possible.

But he knew there was never any guarantee. God already had their paths planned out. All he could do was to put his faith in God to keep them all safe.

And to give them the strength and wisdom to bring Winston to justice.

He glanced at his watch. "Morganne, we'd better head out to meet with the cavalry."

Tanner sighed and rose to his feet. "Give me a lift up into the tree first."

After getting Tanner settled in his perch with his rifle, he and Morganne headed back to the road where they'd asked the state troopers and additional marshals to meet them.

"I really wish we'd found the exit," Morganne said in a subdued tone. "I have a bad feeling Blaine is going to use it to escape."

He shared her concern. "We'll just have to cover all angles and trust in God's plan."

"I'm doing my best," she admitted. "This praying stuff is new to me, but I'm trying."

"God is always listening." He reached out to take her hand. "We're stronger together, Morganne. We can do this."

"I like that." She smiled and squeezed his hand. "And with the additional support, I'm sure we'll get him."

There were a dozen officers waiting for them at the road. Colt used the hood of his SUV to provide a crude map of the area.

"The mine entrance is here at the end of a dirt road. I'm going to sneak up and throw the flash-bangs into the entryway to flush him out."

"Where do you want the rest of us?" one of the burly state patrol officers asked.

Colt surveyed the group. "We believe there is at least one exit from the mine, maybe two. We weren't able to find them, so we need to form a wide perimeter." He drew on the hood of the car. "If the windshield is the mountain, I want officers stationed every ten yards." He drew his finger in a wide arc along the hood of the car.

One of the officers nodded. "Ten yards should work."

Colt hoped these men and women weren't approaching this task from a position of overconfidence. "This man has killed at least five people that we're aware of, likely more. He's been on the run for months. He's armed and extremely dangerous."

Several of the officers looked at each other uneasily. "This is our town. We'll find him," the same overconfident officer said.

"I'm planning on that, but don't expect him to make many mistakes." Colt drilled the cop with a stern look. "Winston will not be easy to apprehend. Expect him to fight, even if he knows there's no way to escape."

"He's the type of man who'd take as many officers down as possible before succumbing to arrest," Morganne added.

He shot her a glance of gratitude for voicing the gravity of the situation. "Remember, we don't know where the mine exit is located, so he could come out somewhere behind you. That's why everyone is wearing vests."

A few officers shifted restlessly, and Colt understood they were finally understanding the consequences of the enormous task before them.

"Any questions?" He looked at every single officer and deputy around him. As much as he'd wanted to protect Tanner and Slade, he knew most of these men and women had families, too.

And that Winston would show no mercy.

"We brought radios with earbuds as requested," one of the officers said. "You and Officer Kimball need one, as do the other marshals."

"Done." Colt glanced up at the sun that was nearly swallowed by the horizon. "We need to get in position. Morganne, if you could get the radio to Slade, I'll make sure Tanner gets one."

"Not a problem." Morganne clipped a radio to her collar and tucked the earpiece in place. "Time to hit the road."

The crowd dispersed, breaking into two equal groups. Colt had little choice but to let Morganne go—they needed every bit of personnel they had out on the mountainside.

But he snagged her hand, holding her back. She looked at him in surprise. "What? Did you forget something?"

"Yeah, this." He pulled her into his arms and kissed her. Her lips melted beneath his, and he wanted desperately to keep her close, but he forced himself to let her go. "Stay safe," he said, his voice hoarse with emotion.

"You, too." She went up on her tiptoes and kissed him again, then turned and hurried to catch up with the others.

Colt took a moment to pull himself together, then headed over to where he'd left

Tanner. The hike was long, but after Tanner caught the radio he tossed up to him, Colt headed straight toward the dirt road leading up to the mine.

The flash-bangs were tucked in his backpack. He paused every ten yards to peer through the binocs–slash–night-vision glasses. Still no sign of Winston, but the truck hadn't moved since he'd first spotted it.

A shiver snaked down his spine. A trap? Maybe, but there was no turning back now. He continued moving forward, using the foliage along the side of the road to hide his approach.

Soon the mine entrance was just fifteen yards ahead. He knelt behind a tree and used his radio, speaking softly. "Everyone in position?"

There was a chorus of affirmative answers in his ear.

He pulled out the two flash-bangs then glanced at his watch. He estimated the time it would take to close the gap. "One minute until deployment. Stay alert."

Another series of rogers echoed in his ear, but he was already swiftly approaching the mine. There wasn't a formal door, just a hole in the mountain, so he chucked the flash-bangs, then quickly retreated, covering his ears and ducking his head to avoid the bright flash of light.

Bang! Bang! Bang!

After counting off five seconds in his mind, he lifted his head and scanned the area.

There was no sign of Winston.

FIFTEEN

Morganne had maneuvered her way into being part of the group of officers who covered the area near the outcropping of rock. She felt certain the mine exit was nearby and believed Blaine would attempt to escape this way.

After hearing the flash-bangs go off, she remained silent, waiting and watching. The officers on either side of her did the same. They were stationed roughly ten yards apart, as much as the terrain would allow.

Colt's voice came through her earbud as he updated all the officers with the current situation. "No sign of Winston. I'm heading into the mine."

Swallowing hard, she tamped down a

flash of fear. Not for herself, but for Colt. He was tough, smart and strong—more than capable of holding his own against Blaine.

Yet her cousin had proven himself to be a cold-blooded killer. She knew Blaine wouldn't hesitate to take Colt out permanently if given the slightest opportunity.

Lord, please watch over us!

Hearing rustling sounds of movement, she scanned her surroundings, still not entirely used to the eerie green of her night-vision goggles. She couldn't see anyone to her right, although she knew an officer was stationed there. Her gaze landed on the state patrol officer to her left. He wasn't well hidden and appeared restless, likely the source of the sounds.

This type of mountain search wasn't something that state patrol officers did on a regular basis. Yes, they were cops, but staking out a serial killer wasn't at all part of their routine. She knew they would all do their best and prayed that would be enough.

With exaggerated care, she eased through the woods, trying to pinpoint where Blaine might emerge. They were waiting to hear from Colt whether or not Blaine was inside the mine, maybe injured by the flash-bang, but as the minutes ticked by, she knew Colt hadn't found their target.

That meant Blaine would be on the move, searching for an escape route.

Darkness fell like a blanket covering the woods. That was often how it happened in the mountains, like a light switch being turned off. She couldn't help but wonder if they'd made a mistake coming after him right away. Should they have waited until morning? No, she didn't think so. Blaine had slipped through their fingers more than once, so holding off wasn't really an option. Especially since they'd gathered plenty of resources to keep him contained in the area.

They just needed to hope their plan

worked and that Blaine would be caught in their trap.

"Winston has been in the mine recently, but no sign of him now." Colt's voice held a note of frustration. "I'm exploring the various tunnels to see if I can find the exit."

It was good to know Colt was okay, yet she worried Blaine could be hiding in those tunnels, ready to attack. To keep focused, she decided to place her trust in Colt's skills and in God.

Another rustling caught her attention, but when she swept her gaze over the area, she saw a white-tailed deer making a run for it, leaping gracefully over fallen logs and brush in an effort to escape.

She paused, leaning against the trunk of a large tree. With the night-vision goggles, she could see another crevasse in the mountainside roughly twenty-five yards in front of her. She didn't think it was the same one she'd investigated earlier with Colt, but it was difficult to know for sure.

Keeping her gaze on the narrow opening, she tensed and waited, half expecting Blaine to emerge at any moment.

After what seemed like eons but was really only a handful of minutes, she inched forward, going from one tree to the next in an effort to get closer to the narrow opening.

The ongoing silence ratcheted the tension to the point she feared she'd snap. No word from Colt and nothing from any of the other team members, which wasn't reassuring, even though they had agreed to remain silent unless they spotted their target.

Where on earth was Blaine? She'd have thought someone would have spotted him by now.

She moved closer to the crevasse, taking care not to make any noise. Anticipation hummed through her veins as she realized this was not the same rock opening she had looked at earlier. It was taller and wider than the ones they'd originally found.

The mine exit? She moved closer, until she was only a couple of feet from the opening. With her night-vision goggles, she could see from this angle that the opening was deeper than the others had been. This had to be one of the mine exits, although she knew there was the possibility the tunnel had caved in at some point.

But she didn't think so.

Holding her gun in a two-handed grip, she ran lightly toward the opening. The tunnel definitely went farther back, curving so that she couldn't see much beyond ten feet.

A twig snapped behind her. She attempted to spin around, but she was a second too late. Morganne was instantly caught in a viselike grip. A male arm curled tightly around her throat, cutting off her ability to scream and making it difficult to breathe. He yanked her backward until she was pressed against a sweaty, stinky body.

She reacted instinctively, using her self-defense training. She stomped hard on his foot, kicked back at his kneecap and reached up to pry his arm from her throat.

But froze when the muzzle of a gun dug painfully into her side.

"Gotcha," Blaine whispered, his rank breath making her gag. "You're not getting away this time."

"Why?" she gasped, unable to believe he'd managed to slip past her. Clearly he'd come out of the cave opening shortly after Colt had deployed the flash-bangs. Before she'd noticed the crevasse, identifying it as the mine exit.

"You deserve to die, for everything you've done to me. I've killed several women since I've been out of prison, but none of them were you." His voice dropped lower. "Until now."

Blaine began to drag her toward the narrow opening. She tried to resist, dragging her feet, but that only made his arm tighten around her throat to the point she thought she might pass out from lack of oxygen.

A wave of terror washed over her. If she couldn't find a way to warn someone she was in trouble very soon, her cousin would kill her.

Colt continued making his way through the mine, forced to duck in several spots as he navigated the tunnels. He worked as quickly and safely as possible, fully expecting Winston to shoot or jump out at him at any moment.

The first tunnel he'd taken was a dead end. Frustrated, he quickly made his way back to the main entrance, then took another tunnel.

How many dead ends until he found the one that led out of the mine? He had no idea—one tunnel often led to several smaller passages shooting off in different directions. He couldn't afford to ignore a single one, which took twice as much time to clear.

The longer he worked, the more convinced Colt was that Winston had already gotten out. Likely shortly after he'd deployed the flash-bangs.

Now that he'd seen the inside of the mine, which was bigger than he'd anticipated, it was easy to see there was plenty of room for Winston to have hidden so far back from the opening that he'd remained out of reach.

Swallowing against a wave of frustration, he continued clearing tunnels. When he spied a smaller offshoot, he debated whether to waste time on it.

But no, he couldn't afford to make any assumptions. Not with Winston.

He told himself that even if Winston had escaped, there were enough officers stationed around the area to grab him.

But the heavy feeling of apprehension that rolled over him wouldn't go away.

In fact, it grew worse with every step he took.

The tunnel narrowed to the point he had to crawl on his hands and knees. Hard to imagine how the miners had tolerated these conditions. He figured he'd hit another dead end, but then the tunnel began to widen again.

Was this the way out of the mine? He moved stealthily, in case Winston was waiting for him up ahead.

Soon he was able to stand upright. A breeze washed over him, and he realized he was close to fresh air, which had to be coming from outside the mine.

He edged closer and peered around the curve. In the distance he could see trees and brush, indicating the exit from the mine was up ahead.

Before he could radio in his findings, he heard Morganne's hoarse voice, barely a whisper from somewhere outside.

"You—won't get away." Her voice was

abruptly cut off, but he instantly realized their elaborate plan had failed.

Winston had Morganne.

Stark fear for her safety hit hard, but he ruthlessly thrust it aside. There wasn't time for that—he had minutes, maybe only seconds before Winston killed Morganne.

And if the guy had escaped through the exit, then all he needed to do was to follow his path. Colt ran lightly through the rest of the tunnel until he came to the narrow opening. Plastering himself against the wall, he peered out through the opening, thankful for his night-vision goggles.

It only took a second to find Winston. He had a tight hold on Morganne, and she looked as if she was having trouble breathing. How she'd managed to speak, Colt had no clue, but he applauded her efforts to let them know she was in trouble.

Deep trouble.

Rather than use the radio, he texted Slade and Tanner to fill them in on the situation and his GPS location. He asked them to find a way to get a chopper in the air ASAP.

But even with help from his buddies, he feared it would be too little, too late.

He'd have to rescue her himself. The good news was that the convict wasn't wearing night-vision goggles, his black-and-blue eyes clearly visible on either side of his swollen nose. Winston was actually dragging her toward the mine exit, moving awkwardly as he held a gun pressed against Morganne's side. Not likely the vest would protect her at that close range, and he had to swallow hard against the knot of emotion that suddenly lodged in his throat.

A moment later, he realized Winston might have known other officers were nearby and was pulling Morganne into the mine to kill her before slipping away for good.

A quick glance around proved there was no place to hide. Moving quickly, he dropped to his belly and used his elbows and feet to slither out through the narrow opening, quickly moving into the brush in an effort to stay out of sight.

And just in time, as Winston dragged Morganne closer to his hiding spot.

“Hurting me,” Morganne gasped. Her voice was so faint, Colt knew neither of the closest officers would have heard it.

“I haven’t begun to hurt you,” Winston hissed. “I’m going to look into your eyes as I choke the life out of you. I hated my mother, but you? I despise you even more.”

His words were chilling. Colt needed a way to distract the killer. He knew Morganne would fight back if able.

He slowly rose to his feet and reached for his flashlight with his free hand. The high-powered beam of light would temporarily blind Morganne, too, but he needed to do something to divert Winston’s attention. To make him loosen his grip and hopefully point his weapon away from Morganne.

Without hesitation, he turned on the light, pointing it at Winston's face at the same moment he shouted, "Drop your weapon!"

Blaine flinched away from the light, and Morganne responded by fighting against his hold with all her might. Colt had made sure his radio was on so that everyone on the team could hear.

"Noooo!" Winston's shout was punctuated by a gunshot.

Fear spiked. Colt rushed forward as Winston turned toward him. Another gunshot rang out, but because of his temporary blindness, Winston's aim was off. Colt heard the bullet hit a tree.

He hit Winston hard, hoping and praying the convict would drop his weapon. From the corner of his eye, he noticed Morganne rolling away, her fingers scrabbling in the dirt, looking for the gun.

Winston roared and lashed out with his fist. The blow to Colt's jaw contained the strength of a bull, but he did his best to ignore the pain rocketing through his head.

The *thump, thump* of a chopper grew louder, a beam of light sweeping over them from above. Colt heard the crash of footsteps pounding through the woods as officers rushed over to offer their assistance.

"Put your hands on your head," he barked. "Lace your fingers together. If you don't comply, I will shoot!" Colt held his gun steady, the muzzle trained on Winston as the guy moaned from his supine position on the ground.

"Hands on your head!" he shouted again. He didn't trust Winston as far as he could throw him. If the convict refused to obey his commands, Colt would not hesitate to shoot him.

Morganne moaned, and his heart squeezed in his chest. Had she been hit? He didn't know but refused to take his gaze off Winston.

A burly officer burst out of the trees,

gaping in surprise at the scene. He drew his handcuffs and approached Winston.

Suddenly Winston reared up, hitting the officer with his fist. Colt was about to fire his weapon when the burly guy threw a quick punch, knocking Winston back to the ground. Then the cop continued with the process of cuffing his wrists behind his back.

Once Winston was secure, Colt rushed over to kneel beside Morganne. "Are you hit?"

She rolled onto her back, and he could see her throat was red from the tight grasp Winston had had around her neck. He felt along the edge of the body armor, then found the sticky wetness of blood.

She'd been shot!

"Officer down! I need an ambulance!" Colt's voice sounded strained to his own ears. "Repeat, officer down!"

A skinny officer came over, playing the beam of his flashlight over Morganne. Colt realized the bullet had grazed her hip, just below the edge of the vest. Her clothing was torn and dark with blood.

"Morganne? Can you hear me?" He'd never felt so helpless in his entire life. Except maybe when he'd learned Abby had died in a carjacking. "Don't try to talk. I know your throat is sore. Just nod if you can understand me."

Her gaze latched onto his, and she deliberately nodded. She opened her mouth to speak but emitted only a horrible gurgling sound.

"You're okay. I'm going to get you out of here." Colt wasn't sure which injury was worse, the bullet wound or the swelling in her throat. Suspecting the latter, he glanced up at the cop holding the flashlight. "Call that chopper. Have them find the closest spot to land. She needs to get to the closest trauma unit as soon as possible."

The cop was wide-eyed but quickly relayed the information through his radio. Colt was hardly aware of other officers clustering around them until Slade rested a hand on his shoulder.

He glanced up at his buddy, knowing his desperation must be obvious. "She's hurt—bullet graze and a bruised throat."

"I know, but there's enough of us to carry her out of here." Slade gestured for the closest officers to gather around. "We've got this."

"Okay, but I want at least two officers holding on to Winston at all times." He needed to know the convict was going to spend the rest of his life behind bars.

"Done," Slade agreed. "Come on, let us take care of her."

Colt forced himself to step back, choosing to take Morganne's head as five officers positioned themselves around her.

"On the count of three," Slade said, looking at each of them. "One, two, *three*."

In unison, they lifted Morganne up from the ground. The cop holding the flashlight walked ahead, and another officer flicked on his light as he followed behind.

The six of them had to move slowly. Carrying her was awkward as they navigated through the woods in the dark. But with Morganne's weight evenly distributed between them, she was far lighter than the pack on his back. Colt was torn between watching where he was placing his feet and glancing down at Morganne to make sure she was still breathing as they headed down the steep hill.

Please, Lord, please let her live.

More cops turned on their flashlights, illuminating the area around them. Colt was touched by how they all banded together to help get Morganne the medical attention she needed.

When they reached the base of the mountain, he could see the red lights of the ambulance and the chopper sitting in the middle of the street. Two EMTs ran with a gurney between them. The six of them managed to set Morganne down on the gurney, but when the EMTs headed toward the ambulance, Colt stopped them.

"I want her taken in the chopper!" He had to shout to be heard above the rotary blades.

"Can't," the EMT shouted. "It's not equipped for medical transport!"

It was something he hadn't considered, so he reluctantly nodded and ran alongside as they took Morganne to the ambulance. They opened the back doors and collapsed the gurney to slide her inside.

Without asking permission, he jumped in after her. The EMTs looked as if they wanted to argue, but he simply flashed his badge and took a seat where he was able to hold Morganne's hand. "Hurry up! Let's go!"

One EMT ran around to get into the driver's seat while the second one began examining Morganne's injuries. Colt gave her the privacy she needed but held on to her hand as the ambulance sped away down the street, lights and sirens on full blast.

Despite his desire to head to the closest level-one trauma center, Colt noticed they were on their way to the only hospital in Jackson. From there, the doc would no doubt decide if her condition warranted a transfer.

Feeling helpless, Colt bowed his head, closed his eyes and prayed.

SIXTEEN

Morganne clung to Colt's hand, struggling to contain her panic at not being able to breathe normally. It was as if she was breathing through a really narrow straw—air went in and out but only a very little bit at a time. And her throat felt like it was on fire, which didn't help.

The pain in her side was easy to ignore. It took every ounce of concentration to focus on breathing in an abnormally slow pattern.

Only the knowledge that Blaine had been caught and arrested prevented her from losing complete control. She railed at herself for failing to hear him until it was too late, but she was alive.

And determined to stay that way.

"I have an ice pack for your throat." The EMT gently pressed a cold pack around her neck. At first she felt as if her breathing was worse, that even the small amount of weight of the ice pack was too much to handle.

Colt's hand tightened around hers, as if he sensed her distress. She wanted to reach up and pull the pack off, but there was an IV in one arm, and she felt as if letting go of Colt would send her tumbling into a black abyss.

With incremental slowness, the feeling of being strangled eased. The ambulance slowed and turned a corner. Morganne figured they'd reached the hospital.

The EMT latched the straps over her body. She didn't like the feeling of being tied down, even though she understood it was for her own safety. Thankfully, Colt continued to hold her hand until they pulled her from the ambulance.

"I'll be here with you, Morganne," Colt

said as she was wheeled in through the double doors.

She couldn't answer—talking was impossible—but she attempted to meet his gaze. Unfortunately, she was moving too fast, her surroundings nothing more than a blur.

Her pulse spiked as medical personnel began to talk over her, shouting off vital signs and other information. She had to close her eyes to focus on breathing.

"She might need to be intubated," one voice said. "Her throat is badly bruised."

Being intubated didn't sound like fun, and she tried not to lose control. She was thankful when another voice spoke up.

"Getting a tube past the swollen tissue will be difficult and could cause more trauma. Let's try a dose of steroids first, see if we can't reduce the swelling. If that doesn't work, we'll perform an emergency tracheotomy."

Someone tugged on her IV, no doubt giving the medication. She continued to count her shallow breaths in her mind, imagining the straw lodged in her windpipe getting bigger and bigger as the tightness eased.

At some point, she realized her breathing was better. Not normal—her throat still felt like she'd swallowed dozens of tiny knives—but less constricted. The rest of her muscles relaxed as she realized everything would be fine.

Thank You, Lord!

Morganne knew she had Colt to thank for bringing her back to God. Her mother would be so happy to know she planned to return to church.

The events outside the mine exit replayed again in her mind—Blaine squeezing her throat so tightly she couldn't breathe, dragging her toward the narrow opening, likely with the intent to kill her.

When the bright light had abruptly come on, blinding her, she'd thought she'd died. Until she'd heard Colt's voice demanding Blaine drop his weapon. The moment

Blaine loosened his hold, she'd fought with every ounce of strength she'd possessed, trying to buy enough time for Colt to get to Blaine.

And he had. She wasn't sure how Colt had found her, but he'd saved her life.

"Officer Kimball? Can you hear me?"

She forced her eyelids open, squinting at the bright light above her. Carefully, she turned her still-painful neck to see the person leaning over her. Speaking was still incredibly difficult, so she tried to nod.

"I should have asked you to squeeze my hand," the kind female voice said. "Don't try to talk. Your breathing has stabilized, but your throat needs rest."

Morganne squeezed the woman's hand to indicate she understood. It suddenly occurred to her that she had no idea how to communicate without speaking. Fear spiked, but then the calm voice continued.

"We'll get you a clipboard and paper soon so you can write notes, okay?"

She squeezed her hand in agreement. Writing notes was better than nothing.

"Here, you can have a few ice chips. They'll help soothe your throat."

Morganne opened her mouth for the spoon and immediately closed her eyes as the ice cooled the flames in her throat, at least for a moment.

"Better?" the kind voice asked.

Morganne squeezed her hand.

"Good. You can have a few more after we've cleaned and dressed your wound." The woman hesitated, then added, "This may cause some discomfort."

Morganne couldn't imagine it would be worse than the hot needles in her throat and not being able to breathe, but of course she didn't respond. This no-talking thing would take some getting used to.

And hopefully wouldn't last very long.

After the medical team cleaned out her wound and dressed it, she was moved from one spot to a smaller, quieter room. Morganne had no idea if she was still in the emergency department or some other location in the hospital. She must have fallen asleep, because when she woke up, she saw Colt leaning over her bed, gazing down at her. She tried to smile.

"Hey, you're doing great." He lifted her hand and cradled it between his. "Don't talk. You're on strict voice rest for the rest of the night."

She lifted her free hand and mimicked writing with a pen.

"Right here." Colt released her hand to pick up a clipboard with a pencil attached. Then he lifted the head of her bed so she could see better.

Is Blaine in custody?

Colt nodded. "We got him, Morganne. And he'll never be free again. As we brought him in, he was muttering about you, how much he wanted to kill you. I'm afraid the man was truly obsessed."

That's what she'd thought, especially after the little bit Blaine had told her, but it was nice to have confirmation. She picked up her clipboard again.

When do you leave?

He frowned. "I'm staying here in the hospital until you're stable enough to be discharged. There is still a lot of work to be done, and we still have several crime scenes that need to be processed."

She nodded, hoping her stark relief wasn't too evident on her features. She knew full well their time together was coming to a close, but not yet.

And she hoped she'd be able to talk to Colt before he had to head off to his next assignment. The thought reminded her of the other marshals who'd come to help.

Slade and Tanner are okay, too?

"Yes, they're both fine," Colt assured her. "You're the only one who was injured in this takedown, and that's mostly my fault."

She frowned. How on earth could it be Colt's fault? She was the one who hadn't heard Blaine come up behind her until it was too late. She picked up the clipboard and began to write, but Colt put a hand on her arm to stop her.

"My fault, because using the flash-bangs was my idea. One that backfired in a big way. Looking back, I can see we should have spent more time trying to find the mine exit, since you were right in thinking it was near the rock where we'd found the shell casing."

His self-recriminating tone bothered her. Shaking off his hand, she continued writing.

I didn't hear him come up behind me until it was too late. I should have been better prepared.

"No, it's not your fault," Colt insisted. "Besides, there's nothing we can do to change the past, no matter how much I'd like to." His expression turned grave and he bowed his head for a long moment before adding, "I'm just glad I was able to get to you in time. Those moments you were at Winston's mercy were the most difficult thing I've endured."

"Me, too." The hoarse words slipped out before she could stop them. This whole not-talking thing was more difficult than she'd imagined.

"No talking," he admonished, but the corner of his mouth kicked up in a smile. "I also prayed a lot and was rewarded when God guided us to safety tonight."

She nodded, agreeing wholeheartedly with his assessment. Her eyelids drooped as exhaustion pulled at her. Between the long day and her recent injuries, she suddenly couldn't manage to keep her eyes open any longer.

"Sleep, Morganne." Colt's husky voice drifted toward her. "I'll be here when you wake up."

She tried to nod, but her head felt too heavy. Her last conscious thought was that despite her best intentions, she'd somehow managed to fall in love with US Marshal Colt Nelson.

* * *

Colt gently took the clipboard and pencil from Morganne's slack hands and set them on the bedside table. Then he pulled a chair as close to her bed as possible, wanting, needing to be within reach. The hospital room she'd been moved into an hour ago was small but private.

He watched her sleep, thanking God again for saving her life. Colt honestly wasn't sure he'd have survived losing another woman he cared for, the way he'd lost Abby.

Abby.

Staring at Morganne, it was hard to remember what his high school sweetheart had looked like. Morganne's beautiful face, her bright red hair, the stubborn thrust of her chin and her clear gray eyes had taken up residence in his mind.

In his heart.

He sucked in a harsh breath, trying not to panic. How had he allowed himself to get emotionally attached to Morganne?

No, this couldn't happen. Colt would likely be leaving Jackson after the next few days. It wouldn't be fair to start something with Morganne that he was unable to finish.

Although, hadn't he already started something by kissing her? He winced as he realized if she wasn't injured and lying in a hospital bed, he'd be tempted to kiss her again.

His phone vibrated in his pocket. When he glanced at the screen, he saw a text from Slade.

Need anything?

He thought of the nutrition bar they'd eaten hours ago. He was hungry, as usual, but he wasn't going to keep his friends from their respective families any longer.

No thanks. Morganne is doing well.

Another text appeared on the screen.

Tanner and I will spend the night at our motel. Call if you need us. We'll drop off the SUV at the hospital before we hit the road in the morning.

Okay, thanks. For everything.

Just glad we got the guy before he hurt anyone else.

Me, too.

Colt slipped his phone back into his pocket and settled back in the chair. He intended to be there in case Morganne woke up and needed something. Sure, there was a nurse assigned to care for her, but that didn't matter.

He was determined to remain beside her, no matter what.

His phone vibrated again, and this time it wasn't a number he was familiar with. The area code indicated the call was local, so he quickly stood and stepped out into the hallway to take the call.

"Marshal Nelson? This is Lieutenant Graves. I understand you're at the hospital with my officer."

"Yes, sir. Officer Kimball is doing well, although she still has a lot of swelling in her throat. The doctors want her on strict voice rest."

"What about the gunshot wound?"

"Just a graze, thankfully. The only reason she's being kept in the hospital is to monitor her breathing." Colt had been told that Morganne had almost ended up with a breathing tube placed in a hole in her throat and on a ventilator in the ICU. He thanked God that she hadn't required those medical interventions.

The lieutenant grunted. "Winston has been locked up in his own jail cell and is under constant twenty-four-hour surveillance. He's rambling about hating his mother and Morganne in a very creepy way, as if they are one and the same person. I think he's mentally unbalanced, but from what we can gather, he's been obsessed with killing Kimball since his escape. We'll hopefully learn more about how he managed that, yet I was told a couple of marshals are coming by first thing in the morning to transport him to a federal facility."

Colt wasn't surprised by the news. "We'll continue to help process the crime scenes, but things should calm down from here on out. We'll get all of our questions answered eventually."

"Yeah, about time." The lieutenant sighed. "Listen, when Officer Kimball wakes up, let her know I've placed her on medical leave for the next two weeks, longer if the doctor insists. She can come back sooner if she's able, but after everything that's happened, I figured she'd need some downtime."

"I agree with that assessment," Colt said. "Thanks for doing that."

"This was a difficult case, and I appreciate the extra help you and the other marshals provided. No way would we have been able to contain Winston without your assistance."

It was Colt's job, but he understood where the cop was coming from. Small towns like Jackson weren't used to being front and center in a manhunt for an escaped convict like Blaine Winston. "Like I said, we'll help tie up the loose ends before we leave."

"Good." Graves let out a loud sigh. "Let Kimball know I'll stop in tomorrow to see how she's doing."

"I will, sir. Good night." Colt disconnected the call and tiptoed back into Morganne's room. She was still sleeping, so he didn't think his conversation with her boss had disturbed her.

The hours passed slowly. Several times Morganne woke up, and he quickly handed her the clipboard so she could communicate. The nurse came in to help her to the bathroom and to refresh her cup of ice chips.

Colt couldn't sleep sitting upright, so after shifting one way and then the other, he leaned forward and rested his head on the edge of Morganne's bed.

He woke up when a tech came into the room to draw Morganne's blood at the ridiculous hour of four in the morning. He spooned a couple of ice chips into Morganne's mouth, then stepped aside so the tech could draw her blood.

Morganne gestured to the clipboard, and when he handed it to her, she quickly wrote, *Have you been here all night?*

For a moment he worried she didn't remember what had happened to her. "Yes, but don't worry. I was able to get a few hours of sleep."

She frowned and wrote again. *You need to rest and get something to eat.*

He wanted to laugh at her concern but simply nodded. "I will, don't worry. I want to be here when the doctor shows up."

She rolled her eyes, then lifted a hand to her throat. "Feels better," she said hoarsely.

"No talking," he reminded her.

"Easy for you to say," she croaked.

"True enough, but please try, okay?"

She grimaced and nodded. When she closed her eyes, he sat back in his chair. His stomach was gnawing at him, but he wasn't sure what time the cafeteria opened and what time the doc would show up.

He told himself to get a grip. It wasn't the first time he'd gone sixteen hours without eating.

The doctor entered the room at six thirty, earlier than he'd anticipated. Morganne struggled to sit up, so Colt slid his arm behind her shoulders to help her, then handed her the clipboard.

"How are you feeling?" Dr. Hill asked.

Morganne wrote the word *Good.*

"Glad to hear it." Dr. Hill pulled out a flashlight. "I'm going to look at your throat." After a long moment, the guy nodded. "Still swollen, but the good news is that it hasn't gotten any worse. We'll keep the steroids going for the next three days."

Morganne scribbled on the clipboard. *Home?*

"Maybe later. I'd like you to try to eat something first. Soft foods only, like scrambled eggs, soup, Jell-O and ice cream."

The rumbling in Colt's stomach intensified, and he hoped no one could hear it.

Morganne held up the clipboard. *After I eat, I'd like to go home.*

"Only if there's someone nearby to keep an eye on you. Just in case your breathing takes a turn for the worse." Dr. Hill used his stethoscope to listen to her heart and lungs. "Overall, you're doing very well, Ms. Kimball. Give your throat a few days, and you'll be back to normal."

"Thanks," Morganne whispered.

After Dr. Hill left, Colt stood. "Listen, I'm going down to grab something to eat. I'll be back as soon as possible."

Morganne nodded and made a shooing motion with her fingers.

Colt was thankful the cafeteria was open. He paid for his meal, then took a moment to thank God for watching over them.

And for healing Morganne.

He devoured his meal in record time but then helped himself to a second cup of coffee. The lack of sleep over the past few days had caught up to him, and he needed the kick of caffeine to get through the rest of the day.

Morganne wanted to go home, but she must have forgotten her house was still a crime scene. So he spent another few minutes online finding a hotel that offered connecting rooms. A place that wasn't close to the mine and the memories of what had happened there. Once he had rooms reserved, he filled his cup for a third time and took the elevator to the second floor, heading back to Morganne's room.

A man wearing scrubs and a face mask stopped in front of Morganne's door.

Emergency lights started to flash, and the sound of pounding footsteps indicated the staff was responding to a crisis at the other end of the hallway. The masked man stealthily opened her door.

The hairs on the back of his neck lifted as he instinctively knew something wasn't right. Who was that guy? And why was he wearing a face mask?

Colt tossed his coffee into the closest garbage can and sprinted down the hall, hoping and praying he was wrong.

That the masked guy didn't intend to harm her.

SEVENTEEN

The sound of emergency alarms rang out. Morganne turned toward the door, hoping whichever patient was in trouble would be okay, when she saw a man wearing scrubs and with a hospital face mask covering most of his features slip through the door-way into her room. He closed the door behind him. There was something familiar about his eyes, but it was the syringe in his hand that grabbed her attention.

No way did she believe this guy was a nurse bringing her steroid medication. Reacting quickly, she rolled out of the bed, scrambling to reach the call light. The man didn't say a word but continued moving toward her.

"Who are you?" The words were little more than a hoarse croak.

He continued to advance, and she realized she was stuck in a corner. Wearing a hospital gown and no shoes also put her at a distinct disadvantage. Still, she prepared herself to fight.

Suddenly the door to her hospital room flew open, hitting the wall with a thud. The masked man spun toward the doorway as Colt rushed in.

"Syringe," she cried hoarsely in warning. Morganne grabbed her IV tubing, darted around the bed and tossed the length of tubing over the masked man's head so that it was around his neck. She felt certain the tubing would snap under pressure, but she only needed to slow him down.

She yanked the ends of the tubing, causing him to jerk backward in surprise. Then Colt was on him, grabbing his wrist and twisting so he dropped the syringe. The IV tubing broke, as she'd feared, but Colt had his weapon out and pressed against the man's side.

"Who are you?" Colt demanded. He reached up and ripped the face mask off.

"Goldberg?" Morganne stared in surprise. She vaguely remembered Lieutenant Graves saying something about the guy being let out of jail due to a technicality and placed on house arrest.

Apparently, Russ Goldberg had found a way to bypass that pesky detail.

"Your fault," Goldberg hissed. "It's all your fault!"

"No, it's your own fault for being a dirty cop," Colt said, snapping a pair of flex ties around his wrists. "You're an idiot, Goldberg. You had the opportunity for a new trial, but you still came here to seek revenge."

"The legal snafu that got me out of jail on house arrest was only temporary. It wouldn't have changed anything. The trial outcome would be the same as before," Goldberg snapped. He glared at Morganne. "And I wouldn't be in jail at all if not for her."

"That only makes you more of an idiot," Colt said evenly. "Because now we can add attempted murder to the list of charges pending against you."

Morganne's IV beeped, and a minute later, a nurse hurried in. She looked frazzled. "Are you okay? We just had another false call, and someone assaulted a nurse after getting access to medication." Her eyes were wide with alarm. "Nothing like this has happened before."

"I'm sorry to say everything that happened is due to this guy here," Colt said, tugging Goldberg toward the door. "He set up a distraction and assaulted that nurse so he could try to kill Officer Kimball." Colt's gaze narrowed. "If I hadn't seen him sneaking into her room, he may have succeeded."

Morganne shivered, knowing Colt was right. With her sore throat, she'd been unable to scream. She wanted to believe her self-defense training would have helped, but if Goldberg had hit her in the throat, she probably would have gone down like a rock. And if he'd moved quickly, he may have even managed to escape without being detected.

The idea was sobering.

"How did he know?" she whispered.

"I'm not sure how he knew you were in here," Colt admitted. "But we're going to find out."

"Well, it was on the news," the nurse said as she shut off the IV pump and disconnected the broken tubing from Morganne's arm.

Colt frowned. "You mean they mentioned Officer Kimball was here?"

The nurse shrugged. "Yes. The reporter mentioned how she helped bring down her cousin, escaped convict Blaine Winston, and indicated she was being treated at the local hospital. There's only one hospital in town."

"It's my fault, then," Colt said grimly.

"We had Winston in custody, so I didn't think to ask that Officer Kimball be entered as a private patient."

Morganne waved her hand. "No way to know."

"You're not supposed to be talking," Colt reminded her. "And I need to call your boss, have him send someone to take Goldberg into custody."

The nurse left, possibly to call the doctor about the loss of her IV. Two security officers came in to take Goldberg away. Once the dirty cop was gone, she was able to relax a bit. While Colt was on the phone, Morganne found her clothes and went into the bathroom to change. After all this, she wasn't going to stick around any longer.

Granted, her throat was still sore, but thanks to the medication she'd received, it wasn't as bad as the night before.

And clearly, she wasn't getting much rest at the hospital.

Colt eyed her warily as she emerged from the bathroom in her bloodstained clothes. "Morganne, the doc didn't say you could leave."

She lifted a brow, but when she opened her mouth to speak, Colt held up his hand. "Use the clipboard." He thrust it at her.

Annoyed, she scribbled a note. *I'm leaving. You can help or get out of my way.*

He sighed. "Your house is probably still a crime scene."

She hadn't thought of that, but even a hotel would be better than staying here. She tapped the note, then walked to the door.

"Okay, hold on," Colt said hastily. "Anticipating your discharge later today, I've already arranged for connecting rooms at a local hotel. But we need to wait for your boss to send someone to pick up Goldberg. Slade dropped off the SUV for us to use before he and Tanner headed out of town."

With a curt nod of agreement, she went over and sat on the side of the bed. There were so many questions she still had about

Blaine's capture, but the thought of writing them down was daunting.

She'd never take the ability to speak normally for granted ever again.

The nurse returned and looked surprised to see her dressed and ready to go. "The doctor wanted me to put the IV back in."

Morganne shook her head and lifted the clipboard to show the note she'd written to Colt. The nurse sighed. "Okay, I need to call the doctor again. I know he's going to want you to be on steroids for a while longer."

Morganne nodded and crossed her arms over her chest, indicating she'd wait. The entire process of getting her discharge paperwork and her prescription filled took almost an hour. Colt met with the security guards holding Goldberg and helped escort the dirty cop outside, where another officer took custody of him. Finally they were able to leave.

She rested in the passenger seat of the SUV with a sense of relief. Being out of the hospital was an indication her life would soon return to normal.

Glancing at Colt's handsome profile, she felt a pang in the region of her heart. He'd been a rock over these past few days, not to mention being an amazing partner.

After riding patrol alone for years, working alongside him had been an awesome experience.

She felt certain he'd be a good partner in a relationship, too. Unfortunately, he was still in love with his childhood sweetheart. Oh, she knew he'd stick around for a few days until she was truly back on her feet and able to return home, but then he'd head out to his next assignment.

Leaving her behind.

The pang in her heart grew larger and deeper until she put a hand to her chest to stop the ache.

She was really going to miss him.

"Are you okay?" Colt glanced at Morganne in concern. She was holding a hand to her chest as if she couldn't breathe. He hit the brake and pulled off the road. "I'm taking you back to the hospital."

"No, I'm fine." Her voice was still hoarse, but less strident than before. He peered at her closely, trying to read her gaze.

"You don't look fine," he muttered, reluctantly putting the SUV into gear and continuing to the hotel. "I'm going to be mad if you stop breathing."

She made a choking sound that might have been a laugh. "I promise, I'm okay."

He parked the SUV, then hurried around to open the door for her. Resting his hand on the small of her back, they went inside. The lobby was a bustle of activity as people were checking out. Colt waited his turn, then paid extra for an early check-in.

Once they were settled into their connecting rooms, he poked his head through the doorway. "Morganne? Do you want to hear the update from my boss?"

She nodded eagerly and joined him at

the small table in his room. He set his phone in the center of the table and said, “I have Officer Kimball with me. We’re very interested in what you know so far.”

“Winston’s buddy Owen Plumber survived his surgery, but he’s still in the ICU.”

Colt shook his head. “I should have gone to see him when I was there.”

“Nothing to see or hear, since he’s still on a ventilator. But the good news is that he’ll live to testify against Winston. Oh, and his friend Sally was out of town and is safe. She claimed her relationship with Owen was only as a friend, and that if she’d known about his helping Winston, she’d have turned him in. We found blood on Winston’s hiking shoes that is the same type as his father, Silas, but we need the DNA run to know for sure. But it looks like your rough timeline is accurate. According to the medical examiner, Silas was murdered about twenty-four hours before you went to his place to find the evidence of his murder.”

It wasn't surprising.

"As far as his hiking shoes," Crane continued, "the tread is a perfect match to the footprints you found at the various crime scenes."

"What about his weapon?" Colt asked.

"We recovered Winston's rifle from the mine, and the shell casings are also a match." Satisfaction rang from Crane's tone. "We'll find more forensic evidence once everything has been examined more closely, but we have him dead to rights on murdering his father."

"What about Kay Fisher?" Morganne asked.

"They found some skin under her nails," Crane said. "DNA will likely match Winston, as her boyfriend Doug Levine has been cleared."

"I assume Winston isn't talking?" Colt asked.

"He was. That's how we knew he'd become obsessed with Kimball, but now he's clammed up. Claims he needs a new lawyer since his previous one died."

"And we're sure the previous lawyer died of natural causes?" Colt asked, eyeing Morganne.

"We asked the medical examiner to review the case again, just in case. But yeah, seems to be natural."

"Any idea where Winston spent the past nine months?" Colt was curious about that.

"We found a fake passport in the mine with several stamps to Mexico. We believe Owen Plumber helped Winston escape, first by hiring his trucker buddy to slam into the ambulance, then arranging for Winston to get across the border into Mexico. Our theory is that Winston continued to grow obsessed with Kimball, maybe seeing her as a surrogate for the mother he despised, until he decided to return to the States to finish the job."

"Did he have lifts in his shoes?" Morganne asked.

"As a matter of fact, he did," Crane said.

"We have a lot to ask Plumber when he's able to be interrogated. He's currently in custody for aiding and abetting Winston's escape, and it would be in his best interest to help fill in the blanks."

"I'm sure he'll sing like a bird," Colt said dryly. "After all, he gave us Winston's location in the mine."

"That's one factor in his favor," Crane agreed.

"Thanks for your help," Morganne said.

"Please keep us posted on any new developments," Colt added. "Meanwhile, I'm going to try to keep Morganne from talking while she recuperates."

"Well, you can't stay in Jackson for long," Crane said. "The protection detail in Idaho Falls isn't going well. There's been an attempt on the federal witness's life. I'd like you to head out and pick up where you left off."

"I asked for a couple of personal days, sir," Colt reminded him. "Morganne can't be alone yet."

"I'm fine," she quickly assured him.

He scowled. Was she that anxious to get rid of him? "I need at least two days, sir."

"Fine, two days. Then I want you back in Idaho Falls." The line went dead.

Colt grimaced and drew his hand over his face. "Two days isn't nearly enough."

Morganne looked at him quizzically. "For what?"

"I don't want to leave you." He hadn't said those words to a woman since Abby, and he felt incredibly vulnerable saying them now. "When I finish in Idaho Falls, I'd like to come back and see you again. Take you out for dinner. You know, like a date."

She looked away, then shook her head. "I don't think that's a good idea."

He froze and tried not to show his insecurity. "Because you're not interested?"

"Because I don't want to start something with a man who loves someone else." Morganne smiled gently. "I care about you,

Colt. More than I should. But you're still in love with your high school sweetheart."

"No, Morganne, I'm not." He knew she shouldn't be talking this much, but it was obvious they had things to discuss. "Abby was my past, and I'll always be grateful for the time we had together. But you're my future. I love you."

Her brow puckered. "How—why?"

The confusion on her beautiful features made him smile. "You are an incredible woman. Strong, smart, tough and more than capable of holding your own in any situation."

"But you loved Abby. I can tell by the way you spoke about her, that she was perfect for you."

"I did love her, but she wasn't perfect. Any more than I am, or you are. We all have strengths and weaknesses." He hesitated, trying to put his feelings into something he didn't entirely understand. "I'm a different man now than I was back then. Being with you over these past few days has taught me that a true partnership is very powerful. Something I hadn't realized. Not just a partner in work, but in facing life as a whole." He pinned her with an intense gaze. "I want you to be my partner, Morganne. But if you need time, I understand. A lot has happened in the past few days."

"Yes, it has." She tightened her grip on his hand. "But I don't need time, Colt. I've fallen in love with you. And if you're willing to give a long-distance relationship a try, then I'll do my part."

If he were honest, he didn't like the idea of a long-distance relationship. But at this point, knowing he had to head out to Idaho Falls in two days, he was in no position to argue. He'd gratefully take whatever she offered. He rose and tugged her up and into his arms. He kissed her the way he'd wanted to do since she'd been injured. When they were forced to come up for air, he whispered, "I love you, Morganne. Very much."

"I love you, too." She smiled up at him. "Is this the part where you tell me God brought us together for a reason?"

"Absolutely," he said without hesitation. "And not just to get Winston into custody. But to show us both how important it is to love one another."

"I never imagined I could feel this way," she admitted. Her voice was beginning to fade, as if all this talking was taking a toll on her.

"I'm blessed to have found you, Morganne." He kissed her to prevent her from saying anything more. "Now please, rest your voice. We have two full days together, but I don't want you to relapse." Her health and well-being were vitally important to him.

"One more thing," she croaked.

He looked into her clear gray eyes. "What's that?"

"Are there any female US marshals?"

"Not as many as there should be," he

said slowly, hoping he wasn't imagining the intent in her gaze. "Why do you ask?"

"We make a good team, remember?" She placed her hand over his heart. "I'd like to apply for a position as a US marshal if there's a spot available. Honestly, I don't think I'll be very good at having a long-distance relationship."

He chuckled and hugged her close. "I'd love nothing more than to partner with you as a fellow US deputy marshal. We'll talk to my boss. I'm sure he'll give you a great reference."

"Thank you." Her voice was so hoarse now, he could barely hear her.

"I think we're going to need to watch movies for a while. Anything to keep you from talking."

She smiled, then rested her head on his chest. Colt held her close, realizing just how much he was looking forward to the future.

Not the next case, the way he'd been operating over the past several years, but on a personal level.

A future in which he'd no longer be alone but would have Morganne by his side, each supporting the other no matter what adversary they faced.

Together.

EPILOGUE

Four weeks later

Morganne couldn't believe it when James Crane called with the news. "Congrats, Kimball. You have been officially accepted into the US deputy marshal program."

She cut her gaze to Colt, who stood beside her listening to the call on speaker, grinning widely. He'd finished his case in Idaho Falls and had been helping her get the house ready to be put up for sale. She'd decided that even if she didn't get into the marshal program on the first try, she'd keep applying until they'd gotten so sick of her, they'd give in and take her.

In the meantime, she'd travel with Colt as much as possible.

Blaine had ultimately confessed to killing his father and Kay Fisher, but he refused to admit to killing women in Mexico, despite what he'd whispered to her while he was choking her. After the DA had requested a psych eval, they learned that Blaine's obsession with his mother had caused him to lash out against women. Initially, he only physically abused them, then had begun to kill them. After Morganne had escaped his attack, helping to get him sentenced to life without parole, he became obsessed with killing her. To the point he couldn't think or do anything else. Still, they believed there may be other victims, during those initial weeks he'd been in Mexico. The marshals were working with the Mexican authorities, tracking Blaine's movements while he was there.

And they'd discovered that Goldberg had been closely following the news, making a rash decision to go after Morganne while she was in the hospital. He later claimed to have suffered a mental breakdown, but no psychologist was willing to declare him legally insane.

She was relieved to know both men would be put away for a very, very long time.

"Kimball?" Crane repeated in her ear. "Did you hear me?"

"I—yes. I'm so honored to become a member of the US deputy marshal team. Thank you, sir."

"Boss?" Colt spoke up. "I hear congratulations are in order for you, too."

"Oh, uh, yes. Thank you." Crane cleared his throat. "I'm very happy Lucille has agreed to marry me."

She could easily imagine Crane's face flushing with embarrassment. She smiled at Colt. "You deserve to be happy, sir."

"Yes, well, I'll call you later with more details related to your training." Crane quickly disconnected the call.

She raised a brow at Colt. "Did you already know I made it in?"

"I didn't, but I was incredibly hopeful." He crossed over to take her into his arms. "They'd be stupid to pass up someone with your experience. And the people I work for are not stupid."

She chuckled and went up on her tiptoes to kiss him. "On that, I can agree." Then she sobered. "You know, it's going to take some time for me to get through training. We'll have to keep the long-distance dating going for a while yet." It hadn't been easy, but they'd made the most of their time together.

And called each other often, during the long stretches they were forced to be apart.

"Maybe not." Colt pulled a small velvet box from his pocket and released her long enough to go down on one knee. She gasped when he opened the box, displaying a gorgeous diamond. "Morganne, will you please marry me?"

"Oh, Colt. Yes." She laughed and pulled

him upright so she could hug him tightly. "I would be honored to marry you."

"The sooner the better," he murmured before kissing her deeply. "I'll try to be patient, but being away from you hasn't been easy. I miss you more than I thought possible."

"Me, too," she agreed.

He kissed her again.

Yes, the sooner the better, she thought with a sigh. She couldn't wait to start the next chapter of their lives. Because one thing was for certain—being with Colt was always an adventure.

* * * * *

If you enjoyed this book, don't miss these other stories from Laura Scott:

Soldier's Christmas Secrets
Guarded by the Soldier
Wyoming Mountain Escape
Hiding His Holiday Witness
Rocky Mountain Standoff

Available now from Love Inspired Suspense!

Dear Reader,

I hope you enjoyed the sixth and final book in my Justice Seekers series. It's been fun to write each of these stories, something I couldn't do without you, the reader. Thank you so much for your ongoing support.

Please take a moment to leave a review. These reviews are critical to authors, and I appreciate every one I'm blessed with. Thank you so much!

I adore hearing from my readers! I can be found on Facebook at https://www.facebook.com/LauraScottBooks, on Twitter at https://twitter.com/laurascottbooks and on Instagram at https://www.instagram.com/laurascottbooks/. I can also be contacted via my website at https://www.laurascottbooks.com. If you'd like to keep up with my new releases, please consider signing up for my newsletter. All new subscribers receive a free novella, one that is not available to purchase at any site.

Until next time,
Laura Scott